AN EAGLE'S VIEW

AN EAGLE'S VIEW

The Days of Visitations and Initial Uniting

PAUL MOSS

RESOURCE *Publications* • Eugene, Oregon

AN EAGLE'S VIEW
The Days of Visitations and Initial Uniting

Resource Publications
An Imprint of Wipf and Stock Publishers
199 W. 8th Ave., Suite 3
Eugene, OR 97401

www.wipfandstock.com

PAPERBACK ISBN: 978-1-6667-3163-7
HARDCOVER ISBN: 978-1-6667-2430-1
EBOOK ISBN: 978-1-6667-2431-8

JUNE 23, 2022 10:36 AM

The Holy Bible, authorized King James version, Corporation of the President of The Church of Jesus Christ of Latter-day Saints, Salt Lake City, Utah, U.S.A., 1979

To family, who are heroes shining brightly.

*S*MACK, the porcelain dinner plate cracks over Joseph Kettle's head, throwing his seven-year-old body forward, slamming his pudgy face onto the cold linoleum floor below. He lies face down and unconscious. After a few moments, with blurry vision, he opens and blinks his eyes, breathing heavily amongst his swirling and muddled thoughts, regaining consciousness. Joseph cannot recall his whereabouts.

"Joey!" a voice calls as if sounding through a long tunnel. Trying to kickstart his senses, Joseph lies limp without responding. The voice cries louder, "Joey! Joey!" Joseph does not respond while continuing to fumble in mental process. The voice angrily demands, "Joey, you better get up!" Suddenly, a quick burst rushes into Joseph's mind as he recognizes the female voice. As the initial pounce to reality digests, Joseph shuts his eyes, feeling a dense sadness overcome him that automatically presses the air out of his lungs, making it difficult to breathe. He realizes where he is—home. Knowing he better stand up quick or else increased trouble will ensue, he languidly moves his arms with great effort towards his chest, eventually raising himself from the ground, swaying back and forth in dizzy fashion, struggling to regain full balance. With caution, he slowly turns around to face his scolding, hot-tempered mother, Linda.

Linda Kettle stands with a hand on her hip while her other hand holds a soapy, broken dinner plate. Her angry brown eyes stare down at her son, screaming, "You clumsy boy!" She sharply raises her finger and points down the hallway to his bedroom, demanding, "Go to your room!"

Joseph shamefully drops his head and begins to teeter back and forth while stepping forward to his room. As he walks through pieces of broken dinner plates scattered on the floor, he sees a damp and faded green dish towel lying amongst the mess. His memory starts to recover, and it dawns on him what happened: While drying a dinner plate with the green dish towel, the plate slipped through his hand, breaking onto the ground, shattering everywhere; then, his mother, who was washing a plate in the sink beside him, in a flashing rage and as quick as a horse can kick an innocent bystander, wrathfully smashed the plate she was washing over his head.

Entering the hallway, a sharp pain rushes to Joseph's head while feeling a small, cool stream of blood running down his neck, resulting from a tiny gash on the back of the skull. He begins to involuntarily whimper. He reaches the bedroom, shuts the door, and cries himself to sleep.

Now thirty-four years old, Joseph slides his fingers over his long, silky, straight, black hair, feeling the tiny indentation on the back of his head, marking and triggering the memory—one of many traumatic child abuse incidents he endured. He is watching television, sprawled out onto a worn red couch in the basement of his in-laws' house, having married for the first time seven months ago. Not having worked in three months, he wallows in a depressed mood.

His five-foot, seven-inch stout frame, which before was once fit and toned, now consists of a flabby belly and shrinking muscles. His face is round and filled with short, sporadic whiskers due to not shaving for over two weeks. Joseph's hair holds a unique shine even though he hasn't bathed in days. His murky brown eyes are soft and gentle.

Mary Token Kettle, Joseph's wife, in a blaze with smoldering emotions, opens the door to the basement holding a laundry basket in one arm filled with dirty clothes. She hurries down the stairs and, reaching the last three steps, she counts in her head, Four, five, and six, because she finds great irony that with the descent in elevation her feelings are inversely ascending towards greater frustration, anxiety, and kindling anger due to the anticipation of the now-depressed scene of her second husband. Her first marriage ended in a nasty divorce after her ex-husband unexpectedly left her for another woman. She steps off the last stair and onto the basement floor, turning and seeing Joseph on the couch watching television at midday. Mary infuriatingly exclaims, "Oh no, not this again!"

Not acknowledging her presence, Joseph pretends to not hear her. Mary rolls her eyes in disgust and scurries by him into the laundry room. She places the laundry basket down onto the floor and turns, reaching up above her to the maplewood cupboard for a new dryer sheet to place into the dryer. Grabbing the handle, Mary detects a scent of urine coming from the food storage room located behind her. Not thinking much of it, she opens the cupboard, grabs the dryer sheet, and places it into the machine. She then reaches into the washing machine and places the recently washed clothes into the dryer, starting it. Turning back around to close the cupboard, she smells the urine scent again. She takes a whiff of her hands, thinking that they might be dirty, but they smell clean. Mary walks towards the storage room to investigate, and, before entering the open doorway, she flips on the light, surveying the room with her eyes. The shelves on both sides are filled with canned food, appearing orderly and clean. Her eyes move to the floor, and it looks dry. Taking a big whiff—Wow, she thinks, The urine smell is definitely from here. Not knowing what to expect, she cautiously steps into the room. With each step the smell becomes stronger. Mary reaches the centered water drain in the middle and stops, taking rapid short sniffs. She glances down at the drain and apprehensively bends down closer to it to confirm her sense of smell. As she approaches the drain and is within inches from it, she repulsively jolts back up, scowling down at the drain. Taking one big step backwards, she thinks, What the heck? Mary moves her head towards the doorway, wondering why this smell would be coming from here; her eyes suddenly become larger as a surprising thought enters her mind: Joey, I rarely see him go upstairs to use the bathroom. Unsure, her mind begins to cross-examine her initial thought with mental doubting, thinking—No, he couldn't. No, he wouldn't, would he?

Mary then marches out of the storage room and through the laundry room, stopping in front of Joseph, blocking his view to the television. Both of her hands rest on her five-foot, two-inch petite, bony-bodied hips as she excitedly exclaims, "Have you smelled that in the storage room?"

Joseph looks down to avoid eye contact and does not respond.

"Hey!" she yells, "Did you hear me?"

Joseph lethargically raises his big, brown eyes and remains silent.

"What is that smell?" Mary shouts impatiently.

"What smell?" Joseph sheepishly responds as he swallows a big gulp of spit down his throat, feeling nervous.

"What smell? Are you kidding me? You don't smell anything?"

"Well," Joseph sluggishly comments, "Not really."

"Come on!" Mary cries. "You are down here all day, every day, and you really don't smell that?—It's urine!"

Joseph looks down at the ground and his shameful face conveys guilt. Mary's emotions boil hot with anger. She glances up at the ceiling and then back down at him, yelling, "You darn, no-good lazy dog! You did, didn't you?" She hesitates to catch her breath and continues, "You couldn't even go upstairs to the bathroom! You had to go down here in the drain!"

Joseph's eyes remain hitched to the floor, knowing he's caught. Like a race car speeding for the finish line, Mary steps forward and pushes Joseph in the chest, sinking it inwards with a watery flow, but not moving his body as it is rested up against the couch. She screams in his face, "You lazy, no-good, little, immature boy! How could you be so lazy as this?" She pauses, waiting for a response, but when he says nothing, it boosts her temper-cylinders even faster, so she continues to take the offensive. "What were you thinking? You are my second and now look at you! Get out of here! Get yourself out of here right now, you little, no-good, little, lazy boy!"

Lowering his head into his shoulder blades like a turtle going into its shell for protection, Joseph begins to emotionally and physically retreat, throwing Mary into even a further emotional spin, crying, "I can't do this! You don't even speak to me anymore! You sit here all day, every day, watching that stupid TV! You don't do anything! You're not a man! How could you do this to me and my child? Oh, my little sweetheart, not another loser, not another no-good loser that comes into our lives and disappoints us!" Thinking about her little girl, Mary's mother-bear instincts heighten and equally does her rage, but as she is about to say more, she notices small tears beginning to water down Joseph's rounded cheek bones. Being caught off guard by this tender emotion, it causes her to pause. Unexpectedly, a thought rushes to her mind— Be careful. Instantaneously, she steps backwards, and her angered feelings begin to be massaged into a small amount of gentleness for what appears to be her emotionally broken husband. Sensing that something might not be quite right with him, Mary bursts into tears, feeling guilty for treating Joseph with such harsh words and forceful actions.

Joseph rises to his feet and starts walking towards the staircase to leave. Stepping upwards on the first step, he stops, turns around, and quietly comments, "I don't think you would understand."

"What wouldn't I understand?" she hastily says through her tears, not yet fully calmed down.

Joseph debates in his mind if he is ready and actually willing to confront his childhood abuse and if now is the right time to tell her more. Joseph softly says, "My upbringing," he hesitates, taking a deep breath, and then continues, "wasn't the best."

Mary replies sharply, "I know that!"

Joseph thinks, Yeah, I've told you a few things, but not everything, not even close. His soul feels tired of expressing to others his pain and hurt, that which he himself can't even seem to fully comprehend. Habitually emotionally shutting down, he tersely comments, "Mary, I'm sorry, very sorry," and starts turning around to walk up the stairs.

"Joey!" Mary blurts out quickly, "You have told me some things, but obviously there is so much more."

Hearing his name said like his mother used to say it reminds him of home, thus pushing his feelings further inward, wanting to keep trapped inside such horror-filled memories. Joseph stands on the staircase thinking of all the unhealed wounds he continually feels within, not being able to escape them.

Mary, sensing his distance furthering, consequently says, "Well, Joe, I don't think you are ready to talk, and I don't think that we can live like this. I want to help, but I don't think I can. I think it is probably best for us to go our separate ways. I'm still healing myself and maybe it's that two broken hearts aren't good for each other, at least not for now."

Before leaving, Joseph slowly turns and looks at her with deep sorrow of another rejection. Then, like a man crumbling emotionally, he physically hunches over, turns, and walks up the stairs, closing the door behind him.

D ARYL Token, Mary's father, is sitting in his work office on a brown leather chair behind a dark mahogany desk, an insurance agent for the past twenty-two years. Every Thursday he routinely organizes his meticulous day planner for the upcoming week. Noticing that his wedding anniversary is three weeks away, his thoughts immediately go back to when he first met and fell in love with his wife, Lucy Oakwood.

They both grew up on the western slopes of Colorado and eventually met in the small town of Montrose, Colorado, in the summer before both of their senior year of high school. Daryl's family had lived in the area for many years because they were generational dairy farmers, while Lucy's family had moved in from Grand Junction, Colorado, because her father received the manager position at the local grocery store. The two quickly became friends.

As summer ended and school began, Daryl was sitting behind Lucy in history class. Lucy, who was naturally reserved and shy yet unpredictably witty, surprisingly turned around to Daryl during class while the instructor was in front teaching about Abraham Lincoln, and whispered, "Hey there, big Abe."

Daryl casually reacted with a smile, saying, "Hey."

"Are you a man like Mr. Abe, honest and true?"

"Sure," Daryl responded, not really thinking much of the question nor answer, mostly only thinking about how beautiful she was with her straight, long, blonde hair.

With a playful gesture, she winked, and their eyes remained attached. Her sparkling blue eyes snagged his soul like a fisherman's hook striking into the early morning catch—surprised and fixed. He couldn't help but keep smiling. Lucy turned forward to face the teacher, so as to not get in trouble. After a minute or two, she turned around again and whispered an affirmation: "You're my big Abe," and grinned.

This was the moment that he knew he was in love. Not only was she gorgeous, but she was fun and emotionally stimulating, grounded in good core values, creating a perfect mix for his appetite. Their friendship blossomed into a beautiful springtime flower as they both fell madly in love and married the day after high school graduation; it was a beautiful, sunny day filled with dancing and joy as their families and friends joined in the happy celebration.

Daryl's cell phone rings and his mind jars back to the present.

"Hello," he answers.

"Daryl?" the voice on the other end asks.

"Yes."

"This is Joseph."

"Oh, hey, Joseph." Daryl says, warmly.

"Can I come talk with you and Lucy today?" he asks. "Are you going to be around in the office?"

"Yeah, we are here working, but you can come by anytime."

"Okay, I will stop by soon."

"Yeah, no problem. See you soon."

"Thanks, see ya later," Joseph melancholically comments and hangs up.

Daryl sits back into his chair, perceiving from Joseph's voice that something has happened. He yells out his office to Lucy, who is sitting down the hall at the front desk because she is the office manager and has been for the past ten years. "Luz, you there?"

"Yes." Lucy answers.

"Joseph will be stopping by sometime today. He wants to talk with us."

"Okay," Lucy responds, and then asks, wondering what about, "Do you know what for?"

"No," Daryl shouts, "but he sounded a bit worried."

"Okay," she replies, knowing that Joseph has been going through a tough time lately, so not thinking much more about it, she goes back working.

Two hours later the office front door opens and Joseph walks in. Lucy stops typing the bimonthly newsletter and glances up at him, greeting him with excitement, "Joseph, what a good surprise. How are you doing?"

With despondency, he replies, "Hi, Lucy."

"Are you okay?"

"Well," Joseph states, "did Daryl tell you that I would be stopping by?"

"Yes."

"Would it be okay to speak with the two of you if there is time?" Joseph respectfully asks.

"Sure."

Lucy stands up from the desk and says to Joseph, "Come on," and begins walking down the hallway. Joseph follows her. As she reaches Daryl's open doorway with him sitting behind the desk working, Lucy politely states, "Joseph is here."

Daryl glances up from his desk and comments, "Oh, yes, love, come on in." Lucy and Joseph enter the room and sit down in the two chairs in front of Daryl's desk. Joseph, feeling nervous, remains quiet. It is unlike Joseph to come to the office without Mary, so Daryl and Lucy have their suspicions on what this is all about, but they honestly wonder what he is about to say.

"Good afternoon, sport," Daryl comments in a friendly way. "What's up?"

"Well," Joseph remarks, feeling ashamed and not really knowing where to start with what he wants to say. His eyes go to the floor. In a faint, sad tone underneath his breath, he expresses, "This is hard for me to say." Pausing to gather his courage, he then stumbles over his words, "We—we—well, Mary—Mary and I, are not—you see, it hasn't been the easiest, it is, um—well, Mary."

"Joseph," Lucy interjects kindly, trying to calm his nerves, "It's okay. You can tell us whatever you need to."

He takes a deep breath and stutters, "We, we, are not going, going, to be together anymore!"

Daryl and Lucy glance at each other and are not surprised by the news, knowing that the relationship between him and Mary was not going very well. However, both are deeply saddened for the two of them, and especially for their daughter, for she will now go through her second divorce in a short period of time. Daryl's eyes turn back to Joseph, and while looking at him Daryl strangely hears an audible voice command from within Joseph, "See our people and go visit Darren." With shock, Daryl's focus shifts to the corner of the room, blinking his eyes, feeling stunned. Lucy and Joseph turn their heads to the corner of the room to see if there is something there—it is empty. Daryl glances back at Lucy with blank, stir-filled eyes.

Lucy inquires, "D, are you okay?" Daryl does not respond, thinking about what he heard. Lucy asks again, "Daryl, are you okay?"

Daryl shakes his head slightly back and forth to gain composure and make sure that he is in reality. After gathering his senses, he calmly responds, "Luz, I'm good," and thinks, Gosh, what happened there?—That was peculiar. As if nothing unusual just occurred, Daryl offers a sincere condolence to Joseph, "I'm sorry to hear this."

Unsure how to respond because of Daryl's odd behavior, Joseph sits staring at him. After a few awkward, silent moments, Lucy intervenes, stating with sympathy, "Joseph, we are so sorry."

Joseph responds to her with regret, "Me, too. I, I, am very sorry, Lucy."

Feeling sad, Lucy's eyes being to swell with tears. As Joseph watches her become emotional, his emotions begin to swim with deeper disappointment because Lucy was the first woman figure that brought an unfamiliar motherly warmth into his life. Not knowing how to handle these perplexed feelings, Joseph brushes them aside, and comments to Daryl, "I'm sorry, Daryl. Thank you for letting me, us, me stay at your house, house, while we tried to get a hold of things."

Daryl states with graceful assurance, "No problem."

"I guess another thing to get through," Joseph says, feeling sorry for himself.

"Joseph," Daryl positively expresses, "We all have things to get through and this, you will you will get through, trust me. Is there anything that we can do for you? Do you need anything?"

With his elbows placed on his knees and his back hunched over, Joseph feebly replies, "I'm okay, thank you. I think it is time I go find some answers."

Not wanting to pry into the details, Lucy and Daryl leave the comment alone.

"Are you leaving now?" Daryl asks.

"My car is, um, it is packed."

"Do you have a place to go?"

"I, I think it is time to go see my family."

"Is that Arizona?" Lucy inquires.

"Yes."

"Okay," Daryl says, pushing his chair back from the desk, standing up. Lucy and Joseph follow Daryl's lead, both rising to their feet. They all walk towards the door, and before leaving Joseph reaches out to shake their hands goodbye. Lucy steps forward, reaches up, and embraces him, genuinely stating, "I love you, Joseph. Please take care of yourself."

Joseph whispers, "Thank you." He wants to say more; however, expressing affection is terrifying and difficult, creating too much vulnerability.

The men shake hands and say their goodbyes. Joseph walks out of the office, leaving. Daryl and Lucy stand, holding hands side by side, both staring at the open doorway, wishing him the very best in the future. Daryl glances down at Lucy's tiny five-foot frame, with tears streaming down her slim, triangular face. She tenderly says, "It's really too bad. He seemed like a nice boy, a good boy; obviously, there is something that boy is fighting too hard against."

"Yes," Daryl agrees.

While reaching up to wipe away the tears from her wet cheeks, she decides to change the subject, asking Daryl, "What happened there? When Joey told us that he and Mary were no longer going to be together?"

"Not really sure," Daryl comments, "but it was strange."

"What do you mean?"

"Let's sit down."

They both turn around and walk to the two leather chairs in front of the desk, facing them towards each other to be close while chatting. Sitting down, Daryl begins to talk: "Well, when I turned to face Joseph and was looking at him," he pauses and then continues, "I heard a voice, and yeah, the voice, it came right from within Joey, not around him or above him, it came from within him, as if Joey was telepathically telling me something. Well, it was weird, a good weird, but, um, yeah, I mean, yeah, it came, the voice."

"Really? What did it say?" Lucy asks, seriously interested.

"It said: 'See our people and go visit Darren.'"

Lucy stares at her husband, knowing that this voice has more meaning than merely words of action. She then asks to confirm, "Darren, our neighbor up the street, that Darren?"

"Yes, Darren Brown."

D ARREN and Rachel Brown live five houses up the street from the Tokens with their three children: John, twelve years old; Roger, ten years old; and Stephanie, six years old. The Browns have been married for sixteen years and moved eight years ago into the relatively peaceful and quiet Denver, Colorado, suburb neighborhood.

Inside Darren and Rachel's bedroom, an alarm clock sits on top of a nightstand—it reads in dim red: 6:30 a.m. Rachel is a librarian at the public city library and is in the bathroom finishing up getting ready for work. Darren is a roof salesman that works on commission and his working day starts a little later. Still in his pajamas, he has been awake since 6:00 am, sitting and reading scriptures in the black leather chair placed in the corner of the room next to the bed. Rachel looks out the bathroom and notices Darren pondering. She lovingly comments, "Sweetie, you are the best."

Darren replies, "Thanks, sweetheart," while still in thought of what he is reading. Rachel walks out of the bathroom to the closet to get a pair of socks, throwing them on the bed, and enters back into the bathroom. Her clean and fresh morning scent breezes over Darren, grabbing his attention. He glances up, watching her, marveling at her womanly and classy beauty. Unable to resist the urge to be close to her, he rises from the chair and places the scriptures on the seat cushion, walking into the bathroom. Rachel's head is bent downward while placing a bobby pin into her naturally wavy brown hair and doesn't notice him arriving. He walks behind her, gently placing his right hand on her lower back. His six-foot, slender, rectangular frame slowly bends down over her five-foot, six-inch pear-shaped body as he affectionately whispers into her ear, "You are my sweetheart for life." He proceeds to kiss her neck twice, once for the memory when they met and twice for the present day that he has with her. "I will cherish you for life, my sweetheart," he tenderly states, coupled with an eternal emotion that travels beyond the mortal memories' veil and into the unknown afterlife, hoping to be bound with her forever. Rachel, surprised by his touch, glances up into the mirror and smiles at him, gently saying, "I love you." Darren moves his head from her warm and soft skin and steps away, allowing her to get ready for work. Walking away, he clearly states, "I love you more."

Similar to Daryl and Lucy Token, Darren and Rachel met in high school. Darren was a senior and Rachel was a freshman. It was in the middle of the school year and Darren was outside the gymnasium resting against the wall, minding his own business before going to physical education class. Down the hall toward the drinking fountain, he heard a few pretty senior girls in front of the fountain giggling and laughing at a young, long-brown-haired girl waiting in line that he didn't recognize—Rachel. Rachel's shoulders were beginning to slightly slouch forward, appearing embarrassed. Reading her body language, Darren's intuition said that something did not seem right with the situation. He immediately stood up and walked down the hallway toward the girls. Nearing them, he heard one of the senior girls mock Rachel, "Hey, look at those shorts—They are almost pants." Another girl chimed in, "Who told you to wear shorts like that, your grandma?" Rachel absorbed the teasing, remaining quiet as her eyes shifted down to the ground.

Rachel was wearing a button-up, pink, short-sleeved shirt with tan shorts ending right above her knees. Her style was patterned after her mother's example and expectation—modesty and class. Her mother always preached that modesty was the best policy, saying, "If a guy only likes you for your body and appearance, then that guy ain't worth a bag of beans."

The senior girls noticed Darren approaching and immediately stopped teasing Rachel, quickly shifting on their effervescent charm. "Hey, how's it going?" one of the girls with a big white smile asked Darren. He slightly moved his eyebrows upward, motioning hello, but that he does not have much to say. One of the girls picked up on Darren's cue and commented to the other girls, "Well, we better get going to class. See you later, Darren." The girls dispersed like flying geese.

Darren waited for Rachel to raise her head so he could make eye contact with her. Rachel, feeling uneasy and unsure of what to do, without lifting her head, turned and walked away. As she reached the staircase to go up to the second floor, Darren shouted, hoping to gain her attention, "Hey, I have never seen you around here before."

Rachel did not respond and kept walking. Darren blurted out louder, "Well, good to meet you! My name is Darren!"

Because of Darren's persistence, Rachel felt obligated to say something. Halfway up the stairs, she turned her upper torso backwards to him and rapidly stated, "Nice to meet you," then rapidly vanished up the stairs. Darren stood thinking, She appears young, but dang, she is pretty.

For the next few weeks, Darren made it a point before gym class to be at the drinking fountain in hopes of seeing Rachel. Likewise, Rachel would routinely go to the drinking fountain wishing to see him. In time, they started dating and dated for the rest of the school year. Darren graduated and attended college for three years, waiting for Rachel to graduate high school. Once she graduated high school, they married.

Sitting in the chair, Darren lifts his head up from reading and asks Rachel, "Hey, do you remember the first time we met?"

"Yes," Rachel says, "of course."

"A long time ago, wasn't it?"

"Uh huh."

"Why do you think we met when we did?" Darren asks and then continues, "Well, after thinking about things and after all this time together, why then and not some other time?"

"You needed to save me," she jokingly comments.

"I did," Darren states with a grin, "And hey, by the way, you looked like a little baby, spring chicken," he chuckles. "You were beautiful from the very first time I saw you, but your hair-do."

"Hey, you stop it right there," Rachel says, trying to stop him before he gets on a roll teasing her. She continues, "You should have seen those side burns and those t-shirts you wore in high school. I mean, what a beauty," she laughs with a pure, beautiful giggle.

"Okay, now you have gone too far," he says lightheartedly. They both begin to laugh. "Oh, good times," Darren states, "You were so beautiful, as you still are. I know that I tell you that probably way too much, that I love you, but sweetheart, you are the light of my life."

Rachel gracefully thanks him and says, "I love you, too."

Darren's tone shifts, saying with concern, "You know, there is something that is still getting at my soul."

"Darling," she sincerely says, "tell me what is wrong."

"I don't know what it is," he states, "but you know the last little while there has been and there still continues to grow an unrest inside my soul. I'm trying to stay focused at work, but it's becoming more difficult; these unsettling feelings continue to creep inside more and more, hard to explain really."

"Uh huh," Rachel mutters, while finishing up her hair.

"Well," he says, "the world, it seems so far removed from what is important anymore. The bigger, louder, more money, bigger stuff, and the four-year degree thing to move ahead in one's employment, even if one has been at the company for a long time and has more experience than someone with a classroom education, just doesn't make much sense, seeming to be all a show, seems a bit backwards."

"Sweetheart," Rachel responds, "aren't we supposed to get as much education as we can in order to better our lives and, yes, the potential to make more money and live more happily and comfortably?"

"Yes, of course we should be educated, but at what cost? We pay all this money for education and then we pay all this money for a house on hardly any land that we don't own, and then what? For what? We live our lives in debt, paying it off. We work our hearts out to earn money, so that we can eat, have a roof over our heads, be entertained, and then pay everybody for it, and the worst part is we keep doing it over and over, day after day—a vicious cycle. Is this making much sense to you or me, or most importantly our children? There's got to be a better way. There has to be a better way to do all this, to make life more meaningful."

Rachel places the last bobby pin in her hair, and Darren continues saying, "So, do you understand what I am saying? Don't we all seem to be living in prison with someone standing over our shoulders saying 'What about this,' and 'Hey, what about that,' and 'Yes, worse of all, what about that money you owe me? Oh, and yes, you owe it to me by the fifteenth of every month.' Doesn't this seem to be somewhat of a prison to us all—to you and me? We are never really free—always owing somebody back and yes, we can't even make our own food and be self-sufficient. We even have to work to go buy groceries so that we can live. Nothing we have is actually ours—I mean really ours. It is somebody else's, and we just pay everybody for it. We are not independent, not at all, and it is starting to bother, really annoy me. Am I making any sense at all?"

Rachel says in her sweet tone, "We have a lot of freedoms. We have the freedom to become what we want, worship how we believe, go to church where we want, and get as much education as we want, if one is willing to pay the price."

"Exactly," he exclaims, agitated, "How much price do they expect? Our very own existence—living free: to make our own food, have our own education, and live in a house we own without working every day just for money to pay it off, so we don't get tossed out on the street. Maybe this is what needs to happen to us all, well, of course, not you, darling."

Rachel smiles while looking in the mirror, saying, "My love, we are totally free to do what we want. So if you want us to go hungry while trying to solve the world's problems, then be my guest. As for me, I am going to work at my measly job to help pay the bills. I love what I do, and we have just enough to pay for what we need."

"Barely," he responds, frustrated, "I know that you love your books and being a librarian, and this has been a great help to us. Without your support, I don't know if we could have made it. My career has not been the easiest. I have bounced around from one job to another. I have received certificate after certificate and have a list of certificates longer than any one of these youngsters getting out of college, but without my degree I can't do what I am qualified to do. And not to mention you can't even get a raise because you don't have your master's degree. Does all this make sense? I mean, in order to get further in your profession, even if you have more experience than anyone at your job, you have to go get more schooling, pay more money to get a classroom education. Sure, I understand that more schooling can help, I guess, but really? I mean really? That in order to get ahead at a job that one has been with for years, we need to go pay money for more schooling—theories?"

"Our kids are not starving," she replies. "I know that we are not rich, but we are making it. Yes, it is hard work, and this is what we are working for, right, to get a little ahead and at that end have it all be ours."

"Well, honey," Darren responds with clarity, "we'll be too old, mostly dead, and senile before we own anything, if we own anything at all. I mean, I just don't see an end to this vicious debt cycle, and even worse, at the end of the cycle, we are too old to enjoy what we might own. We will have worked our whole lives to own something and have it be ours, but when it is finally ours, you and I will be sagging, drooping, and limping, well, I may be, but not you", he chuckles, "too old to actually enjoy what we have worked so hard to have, our own home, our own place without anyone hanging over our head and on our backs asking for that which isn't ours; I understand that this might be comfortable for some and rewarding for some, but just tell me that this sale, this program of what we call 'freedom' cannot be improved. I mean, yes, we have a tremendous amount of freedoms, of course, and yes, I am grateful that God has first given me you, which, baby, we have had some wild and fun times, but, amongst all these freedoms, doesn't our hard work seem to be just for money, to pay for a roof over our heads, and back to your price thing, what price are we willing to pay? Maybe we are not willing to pay the price of sacrifice and going without for a while, and if we were, we would have built our own house with our own two hands with the help of neighbors and friends; and we would have had a house that is ours and not any debt at all, right? Well, maybe except for the price of the land and building materials. So, what price have we paid? Maybe the price of hard work to one day get that freedom that we all want so bad, our own home, own land, that which we can say is ours, really ours, but the price to pay for all this, with how we are doing it now, doesn't it seem to be so binding? Doesn't it? What price have we actually paid?"

She walks out of the bathroom and grabs a purple sweater in the closet. She turns to him while putting it on, and with her big, beautiful green eyes looking directly at him, she says, "Honey, the price we have paid is working hard for what we have right now, and if we need to keep working hard to have these simple pleasures of a home and food, and a bit of entertainment to enjoy our hard work, then so be it. Don't you think that this has merit? Isn't this good enough for you?"

Darren hesitates, thinking. His hazel-colored eyes focus on her eyes with a troubled seriousness. She repeats, "Sweetheart, the price that we have and are paying, doesn't this have as much merit as to what you are saying?"

Darren replies with uncertainty, "I am not sure anymore."

Rachel walks over to him, bends down, and kisses him. "Honey, I have to get to work," she says, "We will have to discuss this a bit later."

"My love," he sweetly responds, "okay."

She turns to finish getting dressed, putting her socks and shoes on, and says, "I sure love you." She then walks away to leave for work.

Darren rests his elbow on the arm of the chair, placing his head in his hand while continuing to read and ponder. His head gradually begins to weigh heavier, pushing into his hand as he dozes off to sleep, beginning to dream: He stands outside in a tall, green, and lush-grassed prairie. The sun is dropping over the nearby horizon. The evening is clear with a calming breeze. He glances up to the sky, and high above is a bald eagle flying over with an elegant and graceful soar. The eagle hovers above in a continuous circle. Then, in a flash, the eagle barrels down from the sky in a rapid charge towards him. Darren feels no fear; he only stands in admiration at the eagle's ability to speed through the air. As the eagle closes in, Darren can't help but stare into the eagle's yellow eyes; they open to a world that Darren has never seen before, equaling the sum of harmony, sacrifice, faith, peace, safety, and hope.

Wow, Daren thinks, speechless at what he is witnessing. He then hears the thoughts of the eagle ask, "Darren, my boy, where are you going? What do you want to have happen to your family?"

Darren doubtfully thinks, Did this eagle just ask me a question? Can I hear his thoughts? What the heck is going on here?

He hears the eagle's thoughts repeat again with more earnestness, "Darren, my boy, where are you going? What do you want to have happen to your family?"

"What?" Darren replies.

The eagle repeats for the third time, "Darren, my boy, where are you going? What do you want to have happen to your family?"

"What do you mean?"

"Your dream, my boy," the eagle says in a loving tone that rings in Darren's ears and seems to echo endlessly.

Darren asks himself, What is happening to me?

"You know what is happening to you, my boy," the eagle communicates, as he suddenly swoops Darren from the ground and flies directly for high black mountains that are in front of them. Moving into hyper speed, Darren and the eagle ride directly through the mountains.

Darren awakens from the dream as his head gently slips out of his hand from where it was resting, startling him. He lays his head on the back of the chair, feeling unsettled, yet knowing that this dream has special meaning for him and his family. He looks down at his scriptures lying on his lap and starts reading in Exodus 19:4–6. It reads: "Ye have seen what I did unto the Egyptians, and how I bare you on eagles' wings, and brought you unto myself. Now therefore, if ye will obey my voice indeed, and keep my covenant, then ye shall be a peculiar treasure unto me above all people: for all the earth is mine: And ye shall be unto me a kingdom of priests, and an holy nation. These are the words which thou shalt speak unto the children of Israel."

Darren looks up to the ceiling and feels that something unique is about to happen.

"**I** NEED you to come as quickly as you can," an unrecognizable voice demands to Eric Upton as he answers his cell phone from an unknown number.

"Who is this?" Eric questions, disturbed.

The voice commands with greater determination, "Come as quickly as you can."

"Who is this?" Eric's voice increases now with rising frustration, not knowing who is calling.

"You know me, please hurry," the voice steadily states.

Eric's blood begins to boil underneath his skin with anger, yelling through the phone, "You stupid kids!" and hangs up.

The unknown number immediately rings back. Eric thinks, I'm going to teach these little boys a lesson. He places the phone up to his ear and with his mouth ready to blurt out some creative expletives, the voice asks, "Are you coming?"

Eric hesitates and then explodes like a pressured rocket rising to a bursting outcome as he screams, "You stupid kids! If I get a hold of you!"—The voice on the other end hangs up. He slams the phone down onto the white-tiled kitchen counter in his suburban Phoenix, Arizona home, next to where he is standing, and grabs hold of the counter's edge with both hands, bowing his back and shoulders upward while lowering his chin down to his chest, puffing up like an enraged grizzly bear. The thought, These stupid kids these days; they don't have anything better to do than play video games, waste time, and goof around, races through his mind as he takes a deep inhale, attempting to calm his upset emotions.

Cassie, his wife, enters the kitchen with her gleeful self. Her short, curly, red hair bounces with every step as she moves toward the drawer next to the sink in search for a pair of scissors to start her craft. She walks by Eric and pats him on the rear end, saying, "That's my boy!" Eric hardly notices her touch or comment because he is concentrating on controlling his heightened feelings. With her back to him, Cassie opens up the drawer and hears Eric mutter underneath his breath, "Those stupid kids. I'll—."

"What's up, honey?" she interjects.

Eric's six-foot, two-inch, thirty-three-year-old muscley body falls to the ground without warning as his head crashes onto the floor, making a loud thump. With her back to him, Cassie reacts, jumping with surprise and shouting, "Wow!" She turns to see what the noise is. Eric, in a seizure, flops uncontrollably on the floor with blood gushing from his head.

"Oh no!" Cassie screams, rushing down towards him while keeping a safe distance, not knowing what to do. She yells in panic, "Eric, oh, no! Oh, no! Please! What is happening?" Kneeling besides her husband, paralyzed with horror, watching Eric violently squirm in front of her, the only worthy action that comes to her mind is to pray for help—a miracle. She closes her eyes and begins: "Oh, Lord, please help, please help, Lord, please help my husband, please Lord, oh, Lord, please." Finishing her desperate, heartfelt plea, she unexpectedly hears a voice come into her mind, "Cassie, I will take your husband and remove from him that which needs to be removed." Opening her eyes, she sees Eric's body begin to calm and her emotions are overpowered with gratitude for what seems to her to be a quickly heard answer to prayer—she begins to cry.

Cassie reaches out to touch Eric, and upon contact Eric takes a deep breath, and his eyelids begin to flutter back and forth like the wings of a hummingbird. Still in panic of what to do and while seeing the blood drain from the back of his head, her thoughts turn to stop the bleeding. She carefully slides her fingers through his blood-filled hair searching for the wound. Her fingers stop just behind the right ear, where the skull is slightly cracked. Realizing that her fingers will not be enough to stop the bleeding, she looks around the kitchen for something more to use, seeing the two blue towels hanging on the oven towel rack. Like a bolt of lightning, she dashes over to the oven, grabbing the towels, and while returning to Eric, she swoops his cell phone off the counter, thinking she'll need to call 911. Dropping the phone on the ground next to his body, she kneels and places a towel over her lap, carefully lifting Eric's head up onto her covered thighs. With the other towel in her hand, she applies as much pressure as she can to the wound. Cassie then picks up the phone with her other hand and begins dialing 911.

An emergency respondent lady, answers, "911."

"My husband," Cassie says, "He is lying on the ground. He hit his head on the ground and was having a seizure, but seems to be doing better, breathing, but his skull is cracked with blood coming out!"

The lady responds, "Ma'am, okay, take a deep breath. You said that he's breathing, right?"

"Yes!"

"Okay," the lady says, "Do you have something to put on the wound?"

"Yes, got something on it right now!"

"Okay, ma'am, what is your address?"

Cassie tells her the address and the lady responds, "Thanks, ma'am, they are on their way right now. Ma'am, what is your name and your husband's name?

"Cassie and Eric Upton."

"Thank you, ma'am, they will be there shortly."

"Okay," Cassie comments through her tears.

All of a sudden, through the side of his mouth, Eric offers a whisper, "He is coming—be ready."

Cassie, feeling a sense of relief that he spoke, is baffled by his words. The minutes go by, which feel like an eternity to her, and there is a knock at the door. Cassie lays Eric's head onto the floor. Covered in blood, she runs to the door, swinging it open. Standing ready to work is an ambulance team with gear in hand.

"Cassie Upton?" asks the woman in front.

"Yes, my husband, my husband!" cries Cassie, while turning and pointing toward the kitchen, "In there!"

They enter and with great efficiency get right to work with a systematic and coordinated effort; bags are opened, gadgets swiftly taken out, and the race against time is on. One woman turns to Cassie and says, "Ma'am, he is going to be okay."

Cassie takes a step back and places her bloody hands over her mouth in shock. She looks away, drops her head, and tears stream down her cheeks as she begins to uncontrollably sob.

H IGH in the Uintah Mountains of Utah sits a rustic and faded buffalo-skinned tepee. Leading up to the tepee entrance lies a two-foot-wide moccasin-worn footprint path lined with eight-to-ten-inch-diameter rocks. The surroundings are alive as birds chirp and dance within the aged and winding tree branches above, while a gentle orchestral spirit is pushing the cool breeze through the crisp air.

With ease the tepee entrance flap opens. An elderly lady who is in her mid-seventies gracefully steps out, with long, gray hair washing over her petite body. She closes the flap shut and faces the outside, standing upright in a perfect crescendo movement from her knees to her neck, lifting her head back into vertical alignment, with the spine causing an upward motion to swing her beautiful hair backwards from her face, landing flat onto her back. She pauses for a moment and takes a deep and welcoming inhale followed by a slow and relaxed exhale. Deliberately tilting her head up to the sky, she closes her eyes and raises her right hand into the air, followed by swooping it down to the ground, picking up a small handful of dirt, gradually releasing it through her fingertips. Standing erect, she opens wide her wisdom-filled brown eyes, and her wrinkled face speaks familial tones.

Misty Butler steps forward with rhythmic purpose, moving in harmony with the earth's heartbeat beneath. Two-thirds down the path, she pauses while sensing something in the near cluster of trees. Two glowing figures, a youthful man and woman holding hands, emerge, dressed in ancient Native American buffalo-skinned clothing. Both have long, shining, black hair. They walk up to Misty, stopping and gazing into her eyes with their solid, keen, brown eyes. Misty does not know them and has never seen them before.

The man speaks to Misty in his native language, which she understands, "We are here to give you a message."

Misty uniquely feels their past: The couple are from many years ago. As husband and wife, they loved each other very much and continue to do so. They never had any children of their own and lived a hard substinence life together. However, their eyes are filled with enduring love and peace, looking at her as family—perhaps a younger sibling.

The woman then says, "Sister, watch for the blanket that will come to you. It will give your people meaning. You must be ready to have it in your arms."

The couple turn and walk away, disappearing from where they appeared. Misty stands in silence, watching the green pine trees sway as she starts to feel weak, as if about to faint. Lowering herself to the ground, she sits with her legs crossed, allowing her upper body to hang over like a frail tree limb, resting her chin on her chest. Her head becomes dizzy, so she gradually lies backwards onto the ground, feeling Mother Earth's cool touch on her back.

Her mind opens to a vision: She stands on the side of a crowded Mesopotamian dirt street that is filled with people that are quickly pacing up and down and crossing all over in a commercial flurry. Her eyes shift through the masses to the other side of the street, searching for someone, snapping onto a set of recessed, bright, turquoise-blue eyes that are four feet and seven inches above the ground—the eyes are staring right back at her. The small blue eyes do not blink. With every passing second her confidence begins to shrink in awkwardness. She lowers her eyes, and as they move downward, she looks upon a boy with a strangely and crippled body, wearing a dull mustard colored t-shirt and brown knee-torn pants hanging from a frail physique.

The boy begins to clumsily stroll down the side of the street. His black hair hangs over the tips of his ears, gliding back and forth with the shift of his head that sits emerged amongst his shoulder blades. His hands awkwardly move from side to side as he steps with unequal hips and feet pointing slightly inward. The boy seems impervious to the hectic crowd as he moves through it with a sense of humble purpose. Her wonder to where this boy might be going surges in her mind, causing her to follow him.

The boy reaches an alleyway, and before he turns to enter he glances back at Misty. Looking into his eyes, Misty hears a whisper in her mind, "Follow me and look at what you have and never look again for want." The boy enters the alleyway. The desire to know who this boy is increases within Misty as she begins to run to catch him. Arriving at the dark alleyway's entrance, she rapidly gazes around to survey her surroundings. Feeling uncertain about its safety, she enters anyway, not wanting to lose the boy. Inside the alleyway, she sees the boy at a distance turn down another dim-lit alleyway. Arriving at this alleyway, she stops and looks down it, watching the boy enter a small bungalow. Her heart begins to feel that something is alive and unique within this boy, so she automatically continues onward. Standing at the bungalow's wooden front door with no handle, she hesitates to build her courage. Then, she cautiously pushes on the door—it creaks open.

Inside there is no crafted floor, only pounded down dirt from years of stepping on it. A thin, flaking blue painted hallway leads to a flickeringly lit room. Everything about this place is quiet. She warily enters and walks towards the light. With every step, she begins to feel a warmth envelop her body. When she reaches the room there is a lamp that is burning out in the corner. Next to it stands a coat hanger with a black coat draped on a hook. In the middle of the room is a small plastic carton filled halfway with fresh milk placed on a dark, wooden, stained coffee table. Positioned in the other corner is a bed frame made of old, wooden pallets resting on top of cinderblocks with a yellow-cased pillow. There are no windows, cupboards, faucets, or running water. And facing the back wall, she looks at the back of a large, brown leather chair in front of a weathered cherrywood desk. A noise begins to sound from the desk's direction. From the chair edge, the boy's twisted hand writes on a torn piece of paper with a broken pencil. The pencil is moving to a familiar rhythm: the tune of family back home. She steps forward. The boy stops writing. She pauses, and the boy pokes his head around the encircling chair. Their eyes meet again.

Speedily, clouds begin to part and stormy ocean waves pound down upon Misty's body. Every inch of her drips with sea water as the history of the world, man, and life flashes before her watery eyes. Gasping for air, a bright turquoise gem comes rushing at her. She reaches out and grabs it. As it hits her hand, it sends a cleansing vibration to her stomach, taking the air right from her. She bends over at the waist, holding her stomach, desperate for more air. With her head almost touching her knees, she notices a beautiful purple flower that is yellow, green, and blue inside appearing from below her feet, which stand on nothing—she is suspended in air. The flower moves between her feet and travels toward her mouth. She starts to feel a tingling sensation inside her mouth, involuntarily asking her to open and eat it. She opens her lips, and the flower smoothly moves toward the back of her mouth, kindly flushing up against her tonsils, and then with a fierce force it pushes her head backwards and swings her body upwards, making her fly at a rapid pace, accelerating with time. The boy's voice then echoes, "Stop," which is heard throughout every piece of matter and upon the hills and mountains that are now below her. Her body ceases from motion and hangs frozen; her emotions stand perfectly still. She blinks and as she reopens her eyes; she is standing back on the dirt floor in the tiny room, peering into the little boy's turquoise-blue eyes.

He whispers, "Did you see? Did you feel?"

She soberly responds, "Yes."

The boy then humbly commands, "Go, become what you saw and felt."

"How?" she questions.

He quietly replies, "Start back with those you love most."

With doubts in her mind, she again asks, "How?"

He answers, "Look beyond the appearance and into the heart. Look beyond my simple room with no carpet to warm your feet, no running water to rinse your hands, and no blanket to warm the soul. Look into my eyes, and what do you see?"

Tears stream down her face as she is overcome with emotion. She responds, "Something of a vision, something beyond words that I cannot express."

He then says with resolution, "Then, you must follow this feeling of what you see in my eyes and follow this with all your heart."

She raises her hand to wipe the tears from her eyes, and as she lowers her moist hand, reopening her eyes, the boy disappears, and the vision ends.

Misty lies flat on her back on the dirt forest-floor path. She blinks a few times to adjust to the sunshine piercing down on her through the blue sky above. She thinks, What just happened? Misty closes her eyes in order to collect her thoughts, and as she reopens them, a man is bending over and staring down at her.

"Are you okay, Misty?" the man asks with worry.

She pauses and thinks for a moment, catching her breath, and then quietly responds, "I think I am." She then continues, in joking fashion, "These old bones must have lost their step."

The man smiles. Misty looks into his eyes, but sees beyond him, into a world filled with love, hope, and a joy that is indescribable.

The man then asks, "Do you know where you are?"

"Yes, right below you."

The man chuckles and then asks, "Do you think you can you get up?"

Misty nods yes and the man reaches down and helps lift Misty up to a sitting position. He gently holds onto her arm and supports her back while she slouches forward. She looks out, and there are people standing around glaring down at her with concerned facial expressions. She pauses for a moment, continuing to catch her breath, and in a small quiet voice says to all those around, "Well, I guess sometimes us old ladies don't have the balance like we used to have."

ARYL, Lucy, and Mary are sitting at their maplewood kitchen table in their home. Lucy and Mary are sitting on one bench, and Darren is across the table on the other bench. Mary is crying, with her head buried into her crossed arms that lie on the table. Lucy is rubbing Mary's back, aiming to comfort her.

"I don't know what I was thinking!" Mary bursts out through her arms.

"Sweetheart," Lucy consoles, "don't beat yourself up."

"Not another one!" Mary cries.

Lucy glances over at Daryl, shifting her head at an angle, giving him a nonverbal glare, meaning, Come on, you better hop on board and say something—Help me out. Daryl knows that cue all too well, but raises his shoulders, nonverbally communicating that he does not have anything to say. Lucy glares with greater determination. In order to stay out of the doghouse for the night, Daryl decides to relinquish to her command and says, "Mary, I'm sorry."

Mary's head jerks up from her arms like a rattlesnake suddenly being aroused from a deep sleep, ready to strike at the next ingenuine gesture. Mary rolls her eyes and says with disgust, "'I'm sorry?' Dad, really?"

Daryl calmly absorbs Mary's frustration. Feeling uncertain if he should try to express any more, he decides to continue and starts saying, "Mary, darling."

"Don't 'darling' me, Dad!" Mary cries.

Daryl smiles and chuckles, knowing his little pistol all too well. He changes his mind on sharing his thoughts, acquiescing to the situation and Mary's temperament, remaining silent as he watches Mary's face stream with disappointed tears. Mary drops her head violently back down into her arms. Lucy leans over with both arms and embraces her. Abruptly, Mary sits up, sighing, "Ahh," and slides off the bench, marching upstairs to her bedroom, slamming the door behind her.

Daryl sits with a soft smirk. Lucy shakes her head, stands up, and begins walking out of the kitchen to their upstairs bedroom, needing some space. Daryl, sitting alone, stands up and walks out of the kitchen down the hall to the study.

7:45 p.m. rolls around, and Daryl walks out of the room. He goes upstairs to his and Lucy's bedroom, where she is lying on the bed reading a book. Daryl says, "I will be back later. I called Darren Brown, and I'm going up to see him. Do you want to come with me?"

Lucy glances up from her book and replies, "No, thank you."

Daryl respectfully says, "Okay."

As Daryl is turning away, Lucy remarks, "D, be truthful tonight with Darren—do not hold back. This is not a matter of political correctness."

Daryl does not respond and walks down the stairs, leaving out the front door. Walking up the sidewalk, Daryl thinks about Lucy's comment and decides to be frank with Darren. He reaches Darren's home and knocks on the front door. Darren opens the door and greets him. "Hi, D."

Daryl responds, "Hiyah, ya young buck."

Darren laughs and welcomes him inside. They enter the living room that is lined with family pictures on the walls, sitting on green cloth couches that rest across the room from each other with a coffee table between them.

"How are the kids?" Daryl asks, starting with small talk.

"They are doing fine; kids will be kids."

"That is right," Daryl agrees, "How is Rachel doing?"

"She is good, thanks."

"And how are you doing?"

"Okay," Darren states, "but you know things have not been the best with this sales job that I have had for a few months. I don't know if it is going to work out. It is straight commission, and I'm not sure if I'm the salesman type."

Daryl responds gracefully, "Sorry to hear this."

"Yeah," Darren says, "we will get through it. How is your job going with insurance?"

"Things are going fine," Daryl replies.

"Good to hear," Darren mentions and then asks, "So, how is Joey doing? Any better?"

"It appears things have ended there."

"Oh, really, so sudden?"

"Yeah. It was a tough one."

Darren responds with sympathy, "Oh, I'm so sorry, D."

"Yeah, Darren, it is pretty tough."

"I'm so sorry. Are you sure you shouldn't be with your family tonight?"

"Oh no," Daryl says with emphasis, "Oh no, it is better we have a bit of time tonight to let some things cool down. You know what I mean?"

"Oh, gotcha," Darren says understandingly.

"We will get through it," Daryl comments, "Things will work out just fine."

"Yeah," Darren says, "I hope both Mary and Joseph are okay."

"Thanks, us, too."

"So," Darren says, wanting to hear the reason for the visit, "You needed to share something with me?"

"Yes," Daryl replies, "First, thanks again for letting me come up here tonight and chat."

"Not a problem, anytime."

"Even though it has been a difficult day for our family and poor Mary," Daryl mentions, "Interestingly enough, I had an experience today that threw me for a bit of a loop. This is what brings me here tonight. I know and feel that I need to share this with you."

Darren sits relaxed on the couch ready to listen as Daryl relays the full experience and finishes, saying, "So, interesting, huh?" Darren's initial reaction is a blank expression while thinking. Daryl then asks, "My question is, why do you think I had this experience?"

Darren places both of his hands on the back of his head, intertwining his fingers, and crosses one leg over another as if in heavy contemplation. After a few moments, he then responds, "You know, I don't know exactly why the voice would come from within Joseph." He pauses and then says, "But as for me, I think it is time that I pack my bag and go find some answers. The quest is beginning."

F EELING emotionally and physically exhausted, Cassie rests her head on the edge of Eric's hospital bed while sitting in a gray reclining chair waiting for him to wake up from six hours of head trauma surgery. The doctors assured her that the surgery went well, and that Eric would most likely recover without any permanent damage; however, the fear and terror Cassie feels inside is not tamed with such words as "likely", which, in this case, reveals a possibility that she will not even consider: losing the only person she considers as family.

Closing her eyes, ready to fall asleep, she is alerted by the ring from her phone inside her purple purse lying on the ground beside the chair. She lifts her head up and reaches down, grabbing her cell phone, pulling it out. With a tired voice, she answers, "Hello." On the other end there is silence. The phone number reads "unknown." As she is about to hang up, a confident and collected voice asks her, "Is he coming?"

"What?" she asks with grogginess.

"Can he come right away?" the voice asks.

"Who is this?" she demands.

"I need your husband to come," the voice states peacefully.

"Wh-," she starts to say, and the call drops. She places the phone onto her lap, thinking, Am I hearing things because of fatigue? Strange.

Mrs. Hampden, the nurse, enters the room and notices Cassie's bewildered expression. Mrs. Hampden inquires, "Cassie, are you okay?"

Cassie stares down at her phone, ignoring Mrs. Hampden's question while still pondering the call. Hidden by Eric's body, Mrs. Hampden cannot see what Cassie is looking at, so she starts walking toward her. Cassie anxiously says, "Wait, hold on. Don't come any closer."

Mrs. Hampden pauses with caution and asks, "What's wrong?"

Unexpectedly, a weak grunt noise comes from Eric's direction, and both women turn toward him—his eyes are wide open. Cassie places her phone in her back pocket and jolts up out of the chair, leaning over him, while Mrs. Hampden scurries to check his vitals on the monitor. Cassie places her hand on his right arm that is covered with a blanket, and Eric blinks, blinks, and blinks a third time. Her heart fills up with excitement as she joyfully cries, "Eric!"

Mrs. Hampden turns from viewing the monitor, and while facing Eric she rhetorically asks, "What do we have here?" She pauses and then happily says, "Well, okay there, sir! It looks like our boy is waking up!"

Cassie's phone rings again. She thinks, Oh no, not now. She pulls the phone from her back pocket and checks to see who is calling and it again reads "unknown number." Cassie says to herself, "I'm not answering this, no way, not now." The phone continues to ring, and she ignores it while continuing to watch Eric's eyes, hoping that they will soon focus on her.

Mrs. Hampden asks, "Do you need to answer that?"

Without responding to Mrs. Hampden's question, Cassie says to Eric, "Handsome, I know you can hear me!"

With the phone still ringing, Mrs. Hampden asks Cassie again, "Do you need to get that?" With still no response from Cassie, Mrs. Hampden comments, "It's okay if you need to get that. I'm right here. Eric is not going anywhere, at least, I don't think so."

Cassie dreads answering the phone, but swipes the phone anyway to answer it. The voice on the other end calmly says, "It is time."

Surprised, she looks at Eric, then over at Mrs. Hampden and back to Eric. The voice very gently commands, "It is time. Eric is ready for his mission. Get him up."

Cassie is dumbfounded. Mrs. Hampden notices her frozen reaction, asking, "Cassie, are you okay?"

Feeling a loss of words at the moment, Cassie only shakes her head no. Mrs. Hampden reaches over Eric's body across the bed for the phone, requesting, "Let me talk." Cassie, aghast, holds the phone out.

Mrs. Hampden grabs the phone and hastily says, "Hello!"

The voice says, "Linda."

Jerking the phone away from her ear, Mrs. Hampden opens her mouth in utter shock that the person on the other end knows her first name. Then, closing her mouth, she timidly places the phone back to her ear and listens.

"It is time," the voice assuredly says. "Get Eric out of the hospital and take him to 1355 Saint Street back home. You know where this is."

Mrs. Hampden can't believe her ears that the voice knows more about her than her name. She shouts back to the voice, "What? Who are you? What the heck do you want me to do? Are you crazy?" She continues, "You better tell us who you are!"

The call ends, and Mrs. Hampden hands the phone back to Cassie. Cassie, now feeling even more puzzled, inquires, "Mrs. Hampden, are you okay?"

"He knows my name," Mrs. Hampden states in astonishment.

"Well," Cassie remarks, "weird, I guess he knows Eric, me, and you, too—strange."

Eric suddenly moves his fingers and toes underneath the white blanket and sheets, and his eyes move toward the door. Both women glance at the door and see no one. They are confused. Eric looks at Cassie and then at Mrs. Hampden, and then his eyes once more move to the door.

"What are you trying to tell us?" Mrs. Hampden asks.

"What?" Cassie responds to Mrs. Hampden's question.

"His eyes," Mrs. Hampden expresses, "They keep moving to the door."

For the third time, Eric looks at Cassie then at Mrs. Hampden, and then toward the door. Through his closed mouth, Eric mutters sound, but he's still not able to say anything. He has not fully awakened from the anesthesia. Dawning on her, Cassie excitingly states, "He wants us to leave with him and get out of here!"

"He can't even move, and now he wants to leave?" Mrs. Hampden exclaims. "What? Is he crazy?"

"I think something might happen," Cassie states, "He wants us to leave right now!"

"Are you now both crazy?" Mrs. Hampden emphatically questions.

"We all might be by the sounds of it," Cassie says. "Mrs. Hampden, the voice said something to you that really shocked you. What did it say?"

With hesitation Mrs. Hampden responds, "It said something that took me back to my roots." After pausing, she continues, "It said to take Eric back home."

Eric begins to make louder noises through his closed mouth. Cassie looks at Eric and asks him, "Should we go home with Mrs. Hampden?"

Eric blinks and continues to try to talk, but still can't. Mrs. Hampden suddenly dashes out of the room and returns with a wheelchair, stating, "I have an idea."

RACHEL rolls over onto her side, holding Darren's hand underneath the bed covers while both are lying down for the night. Darren is lying on his back.

"Sweetheart, how did your conversation go with Daryl tonight?" Rachel asks.

"It went well," he replies, "but I think I'm about to do something that may sound a bit unusual."

"What do you mean?"

"Let me explain," he replies. "After you left for work this afternoon, I had the most interesting dream. And with Daryl coming over tonight and telling me about his experience, I think it is time for me to go find some answers to some questions."

"Well, what was your dream this morning, and what did Daryl tell you?"

Darren relates to Rachel his dream and Daryl's experience. Rachel remains silent, soaking up the coincidental events and possible implications of their timing.

"This is going to sound a bit strange," Darren states with caution, "but I think that I need to go see the Amish people and communities in Illinois. You know that I have been doing some studying on them for quite some time, and their way of living is intriguing; I think that they may have some answers."

"Some answers to what?" she asks, not clearly understanding.

"You know, from our conversation before you left for work, to a better way of life and living."

Rachel rolls over onto her back and stares up to the darkened ceiling in the room. Darren notices her reaction and says, "Rach, I know this is not great timing for our family, but I can't explain it other than that I feel strongly that I need to do this."

Rachel, feeling a bit overwhelmed, does not know what exactly to say. She is tough when it comes to being emotionally sober and dealing with hard things that are presented, but this scenario is pulling at her strong mind, for she feels that her husband is drifting out to sea on his own ship. After a few minutes in silence, she says, "Sweetheart, it is difficult for me to hear this because once I hear you say it, it becomes real. I know that you feel that things don't seem quite right with the world, especially now, and this feeling seems to not be going away for some reason; it is actually growing stronger within you. I know you feel something must be done."

Darren listens intently, for his heart surges with greater love every time he knows that she understands him. He reaches over and embraces her, saying, "My love, I don't know why exactly, but I have to go find some answers."

Rachel agrees, saying, "I know."

Darren lies on his back and markedly comments, "Rachel, I will be leaving soon."

"What do you mean?" she asks surprised.

"I will go to work tomorrow and put in a leave of absence."

"That soon?"

"Yes."

"What about getting things prepared?"

"All I need is a backpack, and I'll take the Greyhound bus out of Denver."

"How long do you think you'll be gone?"

Darren swallows spit down his throat because he knows the next thing that will come out of his mouth will most likely be received with angst. To soften the reception he starts out saying, "I am not sure how long, but a little bit of time."

"How long is a little bit of time?" Rachel demands a definite timeline.

They both know that he is hesitating with what he is really thinking, so he quickly blurts out, "I am thinking at least three weeks to a month, maybe longer."

Rachel shakes her head and closes her eyes in disbelief; she can't believe what she is hearing. She thinks maybe two weeks seems reasonable, but longer than that seems too much time away from work and the family. "Are you sure about this?" she asks with concern.

"Sweetheart," he responds, "Yes."

Rachel feels their hands intertwined underneath the bed sheet and remembers why she married him. He was a young man who was unlike any other boy that she had ever met. He was confident and sure of himself, but unlike other boys, he did not run with common or popular thought, thinking about things a bit differently. She always loved this about him, and now she is seeing this attribute in him come full swing into their lives.

"Darren," she expresses, "You know one thing I love about you is that you never see things quite how everybody else sees them. You look through a prism of idealistic reality—what could be and what should be, and it has always been grounded on your core belief in God and his Son, Jesus Christ, and his teachings to us. You really believe what Jesus taught to be real and not just some nice idea that we should only think about, but that we should actually strive to live; I know that this has been your governing compass."

"Thank you, my love," Darren says in gratitude.

"I support you. I do worry, but more importantly, I support you and also feel that you must go and do this as well."

Darren says, "Thank you. Thank you very much."

They hold each other to sleep.

CASSIE pushes Eric's legs over the side of the hospital bed as Mrs. Hampden steadies him from falling over. With the wheelchair next to the bed, Mrs. Hampden orders, "Okay, on three, we will slide him in." Looking at Eric, she says, "You better stick!"

Mrs. Hampden counts, "One, two, three," and the ladies push Eric into the wheelchair, landing him right in. The women glance at each other, both thinking, Thank goodness that that worked.

"What now?" Cassie asks.

"Wheel Eric out of here and demand that he goes home," Mrs. Hampden clearly says.

"Right now?"

"Yes," Mrs. Hampden says confidently.

"Will they let us do this?" Cassie asks unsure.

"They will put up a fight, a big one, but demand that Eric is awake and that you are taking him home. You and Eric will have to sign away any hospital responsibility."

"Okay." Cassie says. "What will you do?"

"Here is my personal phone number," Mrs. Hampden says, pulling out a pocket-sized notebook from her back pocket and writing her number on it. She rips the piece of paper from the booklet and gives it to Cassie. "Once you get Eric home, give me a call and we will meet up later tonight."

Cassie takes the slip of paper and places it into her front pocket. "Okay," she then says, grabbing the wheelchair with both hands, asking Eric, "Are you ready for this?"

Eric quietly mutters, "Yes."

Cassie and Mrs. Hampden are amazed by Eric's first verbal reply. They smile at each other with renewed enthusiasm. Cassie wheels him out of the room, and eventually they leave the hospital.

Later that night, Mrs. Hampden is sitting on her couch drinking a cold beer as her phone rings. She answers, "Hello."

"Mrs. Hampden, is this you?" Cassie asks.

"Cassie," Mrs. Hampden states, "great to hear from you. How's Eric doing?"

"Good to hear from you, too," Cassie replies. "He is doing fine, resting."

"Okay, good. Give me your address and I'll come over to your place?"

Cassie gives Mrs. Hampden their address and they hang up the phone. An hour and a half later Mrs. Hampden arrives at the Upton's home. She walks up the steps to the front door and rings the doorbell. Cassie comes to the door, opens it, and with a big smile joyfully says, "I'm so glad to see you!" She steps out and embraces Mrs. Hampden and invites her inside.

The one-story rambler home is filled with pictures of Cassie and Eric skydiving, sailing, hiking, and camping. They walk to the bedroom where Eric is lying, asleep. When Mrs. Hampden sees him, she asks, "How long has he been sleeping?"

"Since we arrived home."

"Okay, and his temperature?"

"It's a little high, but not bad."

"Has he had any liquids?"

"Yes, we stopped and got a little drink on the way home, and he drank something before going to bed."

Mrs. Hampden walks into the room and checks Eric's vitals, and everything seems fine, except for a small fever. "Okay," Mrs. Hamdpen states, "we'll let him sleep a little longer and then we'll check on him in a little bit."

They leave the bedroom and enter the living room. Cassie points to the couch and says, "Please sit, and can I grab you something to drink?"

"Cassie," Mrs. Hampden says, "No, I'm fine, thank you." She sits on the cream sofa while Cassie sits in the orange loveseat across the room.

"Well, you have a very nice place," Mrs. Hampden cordially compliments.

"Thank you."

"How long have you both lived here?"

"For about three years."

"How did you two meet?"

"It is a long story, but initially at a work party."

"Really?"

"Yes, really."

"Alright," Mrs. Hampden says with a smile.

"So, Mrs. Hampden, what is your name?" Cassie asks.

"Linda."

"Linda is a pretty name."

"Thanks, I think so."

Knowing Linda appears Native American, Cassie wonders if she is from the area and asks, "Where are you from?"

"I'm from outside of Flagstaff on a reservation."

"I thought so," Cassie remarks. "What reservation?"

"Hopi."

"Oh," Cassie comments briefly, not sure what to say next.

"Yeah," Linda says, "It was quite an upbringing."

"Oh, how so?"

"Oh, little miss, there is not enough time to tell you all the details. Let's just say that it can be pretty tough on the rez."

"Okay," Cassie briefly says, not wanting to pry too much into her personal life.

Linda then changes the subject, asking, "What are we going to do now with Eric and this situation?"

"Well," says Cassie, "Didn't that voice on the phone tell us that we needed to take Eric back to your home—supposedly. I guess the reservation, right?"

"Yes," Linda replies with a smile to Cassie's child-like straight-forwardness. "Has the voice called your phone since the hospital?"

"No."

"So wild, right?"

"You are telling me!"

"The voice," Linda confirms, "said that we needed to take Eric to 1355 Saint Street back home," she pauses and continues, "So, yes, I'm guessing, too, that that means back to the reservation we go."

"Do you have any idea who the voice is?" Cassie seriously inquires.

Mrs. Hampden indefinitely says, "No." She then asks, "Do you?"

Cassie honestly replies, "No."

"So strange," Linda comments.

"Yeah," Cassie comments, "Do you know why the voice would say this?"

"Not really. It is really quite strange."

"What are you thinking, Mrs. Hampden?"

"Please call me Linda."

"Alright."

"Well," Linda says, "I feel that I need to make a phone call to someone that I haven't talked with in a very long time."

"Who's that?" Cassie asks.

"My mother."

M ISTY arrives home to Murray, Utah, later in the evening. She places her suitcase down onto the dark green living room carpet inside the single-wide trailer, walking over to the kitchen. Grabbing a glass from the cupboard, she steps over to the refrigerator and opens the door, pulling out a pitcher of cold water, pouring the glass full. After taking a few short sips, getting her mouth adjusted to the cold moisture touching her dry tongue, she takes a large gulp and then sighs, feeling refreshed. Misty puts the pitcher of water back into the refrigerator and places the half-filled glass onto the tan counter in front. She then steps into the living room.

As she reaches a smooth and comfortable rocking chair that was once her mother's, she gently slides down into it, sitting, allowing gravity to swing her back and forth while glancing up at a three-generational family picture hanging on the wall of her mother, herself, and her only daughter. Feeling exhausted, she closes her eyes, permitting her mind the freedom to wander; her thoughts are instantly flooded with memories of her beautiful mother and daughter:

"Ten years old! Wow, what a big girl!" Misty exclaims to her daughter while her mother, Rebekah, stands in front with a huge smile on her face ready to cut the birthday cake. "I can't believe my big girl is growing up so fast!"

Another memory arrives that takes place five years later: Rebekah, her mother, is lying in bed dying of liver cancer. Misty sits on the edge of the bed stroking her almost completely bald head with a few last strands loosely attached. Her mother coughs and whimpers, then, quietly whispers, "My dear child, I'm very sorry." Her mother then takes her last breath and peacefully passes away. Misty embraces her while sobbing, expressing, "Mother, you've tried, you sure have tried hard."

Misty's mind then jumps another four years ahead, sitting in the cold local jail, waiting for her daughter to be released on bail while thinking with a saddened face, Oh, my dear child, what has happened? This memory begins to bring pain, hurt, and a remorse that haunts her every time she thinks of the slow progression that her daughter took toward drugs, drinking, and a lascivious lifestyle which brought many difficult years, eventually driving a wedge between their relationship.

The rocking chair begins to slow, and while thinking of her daughter Misty says to herself, "A lot of years have gone by since we have spoken." The home phone resting on top of the side table next to the rocking chair rings. Misty picks up the phone and answers, "Hello."

"Mom?" the female voice asks.

In disbelief of what she heard, Misty hesitates in responding.

"Mom, it's me," the voice claims.

Overpowered with emotion, Misty lowers the phone and places it on her heart and begins to tenderly cry, not believing what is unexpectedly happening. Misty hears through the receiver, "Mom, are you there?" Bringing the phone back up to her ear and mouth, she says through her streaming tears, "Yes, is this you, my dear child?"

"Yes, Mom, it's me, Linda."

"Oh," Misty gasps, "My dear, lovely child!"

"Yes, Mom," Linda confirms. "How are you doing, Mom?"

"Oh, I'm better than good now," Misty lovingly expresses.

"Good," Linda says. "Mom, it is so great to hear your voice."

"Yours is angelic," Misty declares, feeling happy. "It is wonderful to hear your voice, too, my darling."

"Yeah, it's great, Mom! Yours, too, Mom, yours, too," Linda states. "So, Mom, how are you doing?"

"I've never been better," Misty claims.

"Good to hear," Linda says. "Mom, I know it has been a very long time, way too long."

"Yes, way too long."

"Yes, it has, but some very recent experiences have happened, and I felt strongly that I needed to call you right away. I hope it is okay for calling this late?"

"Sweetheart," Misty lovingly states, "This is perfect, just perfect."

"Mother, can I share with you what has happened? I feel you might need to know what is going on."

Misty's tears continue to water her cheeks as she says, "Yes, please do."

Linda relates to her mother what happened to her in the hospital with Eric and Cassie and then says, "And the voice told me to take Eric back home to 1355 Saint Street." Linda hesitates and then asks, "Mom, do you remember that address?"

"Of course I do," Misty declares.

"This is where grandma passed away."

"You're right," Misty affirms. "It's where you, grandma, and I lived for six years."

"Yeah," Linda states, pauses, and then continues, "Mom, I think you need to come down here and be with us. Will you come here to Arizona?"

Before responding, Misty gently closes her eyes and offers a silent prayer to the Lord for this gracious, miraculous moment, then, peacefully comments, "I think you might be right. Yes, of course."

I NSIDE the living room of the Token's home, Daryl and Lucy are discussing with the Browns, Darren's plans to leave. Daryl asks, "So, you want Lucy and I to watch over Rachel and the family while you go traveling for a while?"

"If you would be so kind," Darren courteously responds.

"That shouldn't be too much a problem," Daryl says with ease. He then asks Lucy, "Sweetheart, this shouldn't be a problem, right?"

"No, we are here to help," Lucy generously replies.

"I know this sounds crazy," Darren starts to say, and before he can continue Daryl interrupts, "You can tell me that again."

They all laugh. Darren continues saying, "But given all the experiences that we've had, I think it is time for me to go see about a few things. Rachel and I have talked, and we both feel okay, well, sort of okay"—he winks to Rachel—"about me leaving."

Lucy asks, "How long do you think you will be gone?"

Darren and Rachel glance at each other, knowing this topic is a point of tension, and then he responds, "I am thinking at least three weeks to a month."

"Okay," Lucy states. "Daryl and I know about trying to control certain events in our lives. Trust us, we know that there are things that happen that we can never control. It seems like this might be one of those times."

Spontaneously, Rachel stands up and goes over to Lucy, feeling the need to give her a hug in gratitude for understanding. As Rachel approaches, Lucy stands up from the couch. Rachel reaches out and embraces her, whispering, "Thank you very much, Lucy. Thank you for understanding and being a true friend and neighbor."

Lucy sweetly responds, "We love you and Darren, and your family—not a problem, anytime. Anyway, I think my husband helped spur this on after they had their conversation."

Both women chuckle while the men look at each other and shrug their shoulders. The women sit back down and the couples finish discussing things. The Browns go home for the evening.

The next afternoon Rachel drives Darren to the Denver, Colorado, Greyhound station. As they arrive, the station is filled with an eclectic group of people. Rachel puts the car in park and as Darren turns to get out. Rachel reaches over, pulling him toward her, giving him a big hug. Darren assures her that everything will be okay, "Sweetheart, I'll be back before you know it."

"I know," she states, still with a sense of worry. She reaches into her pocket and pulls something out grasped in her palm. Taking Darren's hand, she opens it, saying, "Sweetheart, please take this bracelet that I have made for you." She places into his hand a threaded bracelet that is black, blue, yellow, and white with four red lines through the white.

"What is this?" he surprisedly asks.

"I made this, and hopefully it helps remind you of me and the children."

"Sweetheart, oh, sweetheart," Darren tenderly comments, "Don't worry. There is nothing that can happen that I won't be reminded of you and the kids."

"I know," she expresses, "But darling, a little parting gift."

With amazement at Rachel's giving heart, Darren takes the bracelet and slides it onto his wrist. He says while looking at it, "I love it. It is beautiful, like you and the children."

Rachel smiles and says, "Great. Let us always be woven as one."

"Always."

They embrace, kiss, and then exit the car. Darren retrieves from the back seat his black backpack filled with clothes and food. With his backpack in hand, he walks around to the front of the car where Rachel is standing. Approaching her, he places the backpack on the ground, and they lovingly embrace once more, saying their goodbyes. Darren turns and walks off toward the front entrance. Before entering the building, he turns back around to see Rachel one last time—he waves goodbye and blows her a kiss. Rachel smiles and blows back a kiss to him. He smiles and mouths the words "I love you." Rachel mouths the words in return, "I love you very much."

Darren winks and enters the station.

E ARLY in the morning Misty arrives at the Phoenix airport standing in the passenger pickup area. She sets her suitcase on the ground waiting for her daughter to arrive. A green Honda Civic drives slowly up and stops. Linda, a five-foot, four-inch middle aged woman with a round body and long black hair, steps out of the vehicle. She walks towards Misty with a gigantic smile.

Linda exclaims, "Mom!"

Misty grins from ear to ear, feeling nothing shy of sublime joy that is glowing within her to finally, after so much time, put eyes on her only daughter. They both reach out and embrace.

"Mom," Linda says, "It is so wonderful to see you."

"My baby girl," Misty quietly says through her tears, "You are a beauty."

"You, too, Mom."

"What a joy!"

"Yes," Linda confirms, "it truly is."

After the long embrace and loving salutation, Linda picks up her mom's suitcase and places it in the back seat of the car. Misty wipes her tears and slowly walks to the car, gracefully waiting for Linda to enter first. Linda enters and Misty follows suit—they drive away, heading to the Hopi reservation outside Flagstaff.

Driving into the reservation, they go up a winding and narrow dirt road surrounded by small pine trees, reaching an old adobe home. Parking the car in front and before getting out, Linda comments, "Like I said, he is still recovering—we can use your healing hands." Misty nods okay, and they both exit the car. Linda grabs her mother's suitcase from the back seat, and they walk up to the wooden front door, entering. Inside is a tiny, dirt-floored front room with plastered walls and a worn-out lime green couch against the wall. Linda puts down the suitcase and starts to walk towards the hallway, saying, "This way, Mom," which leads to two small rooms across from each other. In the hallway, there is a strong, natural aroma of sagebrush and various organic roots and herbs that rushes at them—the smell of earthly medicines being prepared for healing. A white cloth hangs in the doorway to their left. Stopping at the cloth and before opening it with her hand, Linda gestures, "Hello, we're here." She then moves the cloth to the side as both women walk into a small bedroom.

In the room on a twin bed Eric lies with a blanket draped over him and a damp cloth on his forehead. Cassie sits next to him on the bed, leaning over him, rubbing his chest with herbal ointment. She glances over to Linda and Misty and greets them, "Hello, glad you made it back."

Concerned about Eric's health, Linda asks, "How is he doing?"

"I'm not sure," Cassie responds. "His temperature seems to be rising a bit, and he still continues to rest."

"Alright," Linda says. "We got the right woman with us now to help." Linda puts her arm around her mother's shoulder and introduces her, "Cassie, this is my mom, Misty."

Cassie smiles warmly and says, "Oh, so glad to meet you and so great that you made it. We have been waiting for you. How was the trip in?"

Misty grins at her kindness and answers, "Cassie, great to meet you as well and it was good. We made it in good time, at least I think we did."

"Good," Cassie states, "Linda has told me all about you and I'm excited to get to know you."

"Me, too," Misty genuinely says. "Let's see if we can help here a bit. Do you mind if I see what we are dealing with?"

Cassie respectfully replies, "Please. Linda did say that you have a gift with healing."

"I'm not so sure about that, but sometimes us old folks get a bit lucky at times."

Cassie grins and then asks, "I'm guessing Linda told you all about us and Eric?"

"Yes, Linda told me the situation on the drive out here. How has his breathing been the last little while?"

"I think okay, but they are short, little breaths, like he is extremely tired."

"Okay," Misty says, "Has he opened his eyes lately?"

"No, it has been a while, maybe since last night when we brought him here and a few times early this morning."

"Alright." Misty steps forward and Cassie stands up, backing away. Misty stands, initially overlooking Eric, and then asks, "Has there been a prayer done for him?"

Linda and Cassie both shake their heads no. Misty claims with humility, "Then, I suggest that we first offer one."

They all three stand next to one another in a circle, holding hands. Misty offers a prayer in her native Ute tongue. When she is finished Cassie sincerely comments, "Thank you."

"No problem. It usually helps when he," Misty lifts her eyes to the ceiling, "is involved."

"Mom," Linda interrupts, "I bet you are hungry. Before you actually get started, do you want a little bite to eat?"

"Yeah, that actually would be nice," Misty remarks.

"Cassie," Linda asks, "Do you want something to eat?"

"No, thank you."

"Alright, suit yourself," Linda says, and both she and Misty walk out of the room across the hallway and into the small kitchen. Linda prepares Misty a peanut butter and honey sandwich with a glass of water to drink.

While eating her sandwich Misty asks, "So, what is next?"

Linda's phone begins to ring. She looks down at the phone number and it reads—"unknown number." She frankly states, "We're about to find out," and answers the call. "Hello."

The voice on the other end asks, "Are you coming?"

"Are we coming?" Linda asks rhetorically, feeling annoyed by the unknown voice.

"Yes, we are waiting for you."

"How do you know us?"

"Please bring Eric with you and now, bring your mother also."

"Who is this?" Misty demands in frustration.

"We are waiting for all of you to come—It is time."

The phone hangs up. Linda looks at her mother and says angrily, "Who are these people that keep calling? They called Cassie's phone and now they have my phone number. They now know that you are here."

"What?" Misty inquires, not understanding what her daughter is talking about.

"Yes, they now know that you are here. They said that they are waiting for all of us to come; they even said—You: they know that you are here and that you are my mother. What the heck?"

Misty remembers the boy's eyes she saw in her vision—they were so soft, calm, loving, and kind. She knows that whoever called they must go and see.

A	FTER changing his destination last-minute, Darren awakes in the Greyhound station from sleeping there overnight. He stands up, grabs his bag, and goes to the restroom to clean up. Leaving the bathroom, he walks to the passenger line to board the bus. Reaching the bus, Darren hands the Greyhound bus ticket to the driver and places his backpack down on the ground next to the side of the bus so it can be stowed away underneath in the baggage carrier. Darren walks up the steps, entering the bus. Seeing an empty row in the middle, he walks towards it and sits down in the window seat.

After a few minutes, a large and robust Native American man enters the bus. His chest and shoulders tower over the passengers below, and his cheeks are unusually long and sleek, like his black, shiny hair that is braided down to the middle of his back. He is wearing a short-sleeved, blue, collared shirt with a black vest and denim jeans. Hanging from his neck is an intricately patterned and meticulously detailed beaded necklace with a circular emblem dangling at the bottom consisting of turquoise, white, and shades of blue colors intertwined. The man is carrying a navy blue handbag. He walks up to the row across the aisle from Darren because it is open. Darren gestures with a smile and the man smiles back. The man gently places the bag on the ground in front of the window seat and sits down in the aisle seat.

The bus driver stands at the front of the bus and picks up the microphone, saying with great enthusiasm, "Good morning, ladies and gentlemen, and thanks for riding Greyhound this fine, how-do-you-do day!" He pauses and continues, "Well, if you weren't awake, now you are! Please have your tickets in hand, and I will walk down the aisle making sure we are all on the right bus and correct connection!" After checking all the passengers' tickets, the bus driver sits down behind the wheel and drives out of the station.

With great curiosity about the Native American man across the aisle, Darren can't help but keep glancing at him from the corner of his eye. The man catches Darren's eyes and nods at him as if to say, "I see you, why do you keep looking over here?" Darren looks over at him and nods, copying the man's gesture. Deciding he better break the ice or else it might get awkward soon, Darren says with a gentle smile, "Hello, not too crowded, nice, huh?"

The man hesitates before responding and unusually scans the premises with his eyes. He then quietly replies, "Yeah."

"So, where are you headed?" Darren asks.

Again hesitating, the man quickly replies, "Arizona."

"Oh, me, too."

The man nods okay. Darren wonders if he should keep prying, but his intrigue outweighs the awareness of the man's reluctancy in responding. So Darren pushes onward, "What's taking you to Arizona?"

"See my grandparents," the man states frankly.

"They must be quite old?"

"No, dead."

"What?" Darren asks with astonishment.

The man begins to slightly grin.

"Oh," Darren says, smiling, aware that the man is possibly being sarcastic, but maybe not entirely. Not sure what to say next, Darren plays along, "Well, I hope you see them."

The man smiles wider and freely remarks, "Oh, you white folks are so funny."

"I'm sure we are," Darren says, feeling uncertain how to take the comment. However, feeling drawn towards this man for some odd reason and not wanting to give up on the conversation, Darren decides to let any and all offensive implications that could be derived from the man's previous comment go; pushing onward, he asks, "Are you from Arizona?"

The man nods yes.

"What part?"

"Grand Canyon."

"Beautiful," Darren expresses, "Went there as a family some time ago."

"Did you like it?"

"Unbelievable."

"If you only knew."

Darren pauses, feeling that what he just said comes with more meaning than merely words.

The man then asks Darren, "Why Arizona?"

"Well, my final destination is actually Illinois, the land of Lincoln, where I have a few Amish friends that I am going to see, but interestingly, I felt strongly that I needed to first go down to the Grand Canyon area."

"Interesting," the man says, pauses, and then declares, "The Amish are peculiarly similar to us."

"How?" Darren asks, interested in the man's point of view.

"With a few things," the man initially responds, smiling and winking as if he knows something that Darren is completely unaware of. "First, they try darn hard to not separate their spiritual and religious beliefs from their livelihood. And secondly, they live within the American governmental and political framework, but remain as their own believing communities." The man then asks, "Why the Grand Canyon?"

"Not sure."

"Interesting," the man remarks again with a grin.

"It is," Darren says, "isn't it?"

"Maybe more than we know," tersely, the man replies.

Feeling compelled to share, Darren states, "This is going to sound a bit strange, but with some recent experiences that have happened there appear to be more questions within my soul than answers right now."

"Interesting," the man says for the third time and asks, "what questions?"

With not many people seeming to care about Darren's recent tumultuous feelings cemented in deep concern for the world and things going on around him, he suddenly feels grateful for the man's ostensibly sincere curiosity, even if it is from a stranger. Feeling rushed at the opportunity to express himself to a willing listener, Darren takes a deep breath to first slow his thoughts down. He clearly states, "First, the world appears to be spiritually decaying. The love of God and of man seem to be going cold. Furthermore, things are noticeably upside down, inside out, and backwards. This confronts me with the question if, indeed, there is a better way to live than what we are doing currently."

The man sits, still looking forward, and then calmly offers the most simple and logical follow-up question, "Why are you feeling this way?"

With seriousness, Darren responds, "Because our people seem to be moving toward unjust violence and increased immorality—hatred is brewing in the heart of man."

"Interesting," the man states for the fourth time while sensing Darren's intense disappointment with things. Allowing the dust to settle and any truth particle to be rooted, the man pauses and then inquires, "So, what are you hoping to find?"

Darren turns toward him from glancing out the window and directly responds, "Answers."

The man nods his head up and down as if he clearly understands, quietly remarking, "I see."

"We all seem to be chasing something that can never actually be attained," Darren strongly asserts.

"What are we trying to obtain?"

"Spiritual freedom, liberty, peace, love, and harmony with one another."

"And what does all this look like?" poignantly, the man asks.

Darren hesitates to respond because he knows that he is uncertain of the answer to this man's digging. Not wanting to sound like a person without a thinking brain, he doubtfully responds, "I have some ideas."

"What are they?" the man inquires. "What are your solutions?"

Again, Darren pauses, knowing that his own problem-solving ideas to his increasing inner dilemma are still premature and developing, thus a cause to feel compelled to search for more answers. However, in order to change the serious atmosphere and hoping to lighten the mood, he changes the subject, asking, "By the way, what is your name?"

"Robert," the man replies.

Darren reaches out his hand and jovially says, "Robert, Darren Brown, good to meet you." Robert reaches over and says, "Robert Hanson." They shake hands.

As they let go of each other's hands, the bus slams on the brakes, throwing both men forward, crashing into the back of the seats in front of them. The bus comes to a screeching stop. Darren glances over at Robert to make sure that he is okay. Robert is reaching into his bag, pulling out a palm-sized object. He then reaches over the aisle to Darren with his fist closed and hand facing down, rapidly saying, "I need you to keep this. Can you do this for me?"

Darren gazes down at his fist wondering what is happening and what is inside. Uncertain about what action to take, he is frozen in thought.

"Will you keep this for me?" asks Robert, intensely.

Still unsure what to do and mentally paralyzed by the sudden rush of events, Darren shakes his head no. Robert dismisses Darren's reaction and quickly leans further toward him, prying open his hand, saying, "Please keep this safe!" He drops a palm-sized silver medallion into Darren's hand. Darren glances down at the medallion and is shocked by its archaic appearance. He quickly closes his hand and places it in his left gray sweater pocket, which is rolled up on his lap.

The bus door opens and two male cops enter, holding and pointing handguns forward as they move up the steps. The first cop reaches the aisle and yells to the passengers, "Nobody move!" He begins to walk down the aisle, surveying each passenger while the other cop stands behind, pointing his gun toward the onlookers, protecting his partner. He reaches Robert, stopping, and while pointing the gun directly at him, he asks, "Do you have it?"

Robert calmly responds, "Yes."

"Where is it?" The cop asks, demanding a quick answer.

"In my bag," Robert states as his eyes move down to the navy-blue handbag on the floor.

"Keep your hands where I can see them," the cop commands, "and retrieve the bag very slowly—very slowly!"

Robert deliberately raises his palms to the officer, and then reaches down with his right hand to collect the bag. He grabs the bag and places it on his lap. The cop asks, "Is that everything?"

Robert nods yes.

"Get off the bus, now, and slowly," the cop orders.

Robert gradually stands up with the bag in his hand. The cop starts to walk backward, facing Robert and pointing the gun directly at his chest as Robert walks forward. Robert and the cops walk off the bus. Darren, sitting in his seat in pure astonishment, quickly stands up and moves across the aisle to look out the window to witness what is happening. Robert is escorted into the back seat of a black car. The car squeals off down the road.

Darren sits back down into his seat and breathes heavily while his heart is racing. He thinks, What in the heck was that all about? The bus driver announces overhead, "Ladies and gentleman, thank you for all being calm. I'm very sorry about the interruption. We will continue now to our next stop, Grand Junction."

Reaching down over the sweater's front pocket from the outside, Darren feels the medallion, making sure that it is secure. Fearful of taking it out of the sweater, Darren initially glances all around for unwanted eyes. He then scoots down into his seat, trying to be less visible. Cautiously reaching into his sweater pocket, he pulls out the medallion. No bigger than his palm, he feels its contoured edges on his skin. He turns his palm up and slowly opens his fingers. His eyes first catch hold of the repeating, thin, diminishing lines moving inward to the center, representing the sun's rays. Following the lines inward, four angels fly with wings stretched out in each cardinal direction, guarding what is in the center—a single eye. Darren flips the medallion over to investigate the back. There are two numbers faintly etched, 33. Not wanting to keep it out in the open much longer, he gently places the medallion back into the sweater and places it under his left arm, which is resting under the window. Wondering what the significance might be with this small medallion, Darren's eyes begin to become sleepy and his head sluggishly drops, falling asleep.

D ARYL and Lucy walk up the street to check on Rachel and the kids. Lucy comments, "I hope that Darren is okay and will be okay."

Daryl, standing six feet and two inches tall, looks down at Lucy, who is five feet tall, and states, "Sweetheart, it will all work out."

Lucy replies, "Why can't things work out another way—more normal?"

"Love," Daryl says, "you know some things we perceive as normal are sometimes our own perceptions, judgments, and biases. And sometimes things need to be abnormal for the normal to be moved, checked, or altered a bit, making us think and live differently."

They arrive at the door and knock. Rachel opens the door, and upon seeing them she quickly steps out and gives them both a hug, saying, "Oh, I'm grateful to see both of you two today. I know he only left yesterday, but I am sure glad to see you guys. Come on in."

Daryl and Lucy enter the house and follow Rachel into the kitchen where the kids are at the table, doing homework. When Stephanie sees Daryl, she runs up to him, giving him a big hug. While holding her, Daryl joyfully asks, "How's my girl doing?"

"Good," she replies, giving him a tighter squeeze.

Glancing down at the boys, Daryl says, "Hey, boys!"

"Hey, big D!" they both respond, enthusiastically.

"That's right, don't you forget it!"

The boys chuckle. With Stephanie still in his arms, Daryl glimpses behind the boys at a large painting hanging on the wall,

The Calm Sea by Gustave Courbet. He confidently declares, "Great painting!"

"You always say this every time you come in here," Rachel says. "This is one of Darren's favorites."

"You always say that when I come in here," Daryl repeats while smiling at her. She smiles back at his timely sense of humor. "Again, why Courbet?"

"I really don't know," Rachel states, "but he just loves all kinds of paintings and the arts."

"Hum, I knew he was a bit different," Daryl jokes, then waits for Rachel to smile, and when he gets his desired reaction, he then says, "But not that different."

Lucy then asks, "I can't remember, is Darren an artist? Does he paint as well?"

"He loves to paint when he can, but not much time around here for that."

"Well, that is really neat," Lucy says.

"Yeah, it is," Rachel says. "Please sit down and join us."

Daryl puts Stephanie down, and he and Lucy sit down at the table. Lucy asks, "How did it go yesterday at the bus station?"

"I think it went okay," Rachel states, "but just nervous a bit and a little sad to have him go."

"I bet," Lucy comments. "We came by to make sure you are all okay."

"Thank you," Rachel gratefully states. She walks around the counter with glasses of water in her hands. She places the cups in front of Daryl and Lucy and sits down at the table. With grace, Rachel says, "Thank you so much for the both of you being so kind and willing to help our family during this unusual time. I know this is not very normal, a bit weird, but it is much appreciated."

Lucy smiles at her while Daryl, not paying attention to the conversation, is focused on the painting on the wall because something doesn't seem right to him. Struggling to know what it is, he squints, turning his head slightly in thought. He is familiar with the painting because it was also his grandfather's favorite painting and had it placed in his house. While looking at the painting, Daryl's thoughts are taken back to his childhood when he was twelve years old. He is standing in the living room of his grandfather's house listening to him talk with an old friend about the painting:

"This painting moves me on a side that many people cannot touch," his grandfather states.

"You're strange. What the heck do you mean?" the friend probes.

"Look!" the grandfather commands. "The shore and the boats, calming reassurance, exquisitely peaceful."

"Really?" his old friend asks with disdain. "Where do you see that?"

"Are you blind?" The grandfather, annoyed, sarcastically asks.

"Half blind, but what does that have to do with anything?"

"That's what I thought. Only a blind man would say such a thing as this!"

"You are the one that might be blind!" the friend jokes.

"Will you look at those boats!" The grandfather demands with emphasis.

Sitting at the table, Daryl's eyes shift to focus on the boats in the painting.

"Daryl," Lucy says, hoping to grab his attention, "Are you with us?"

"Yeah, all here, sweetheart!" Daryl affirms while still peering up, perplexed at the painting. He says to himself, "The boats, there appears to be an extra, smaller boat in the background in the right corner." He leans forward and squints harder. By this time, everyone around the table is glaring up at the painting, even the children.

"Look at the right corner!" Daryl suddenly exclaims. "Look!" Daryl stands up and walks up to the painting. Pointing at the right bottom, he turns to everyone and says, "Look! He hesitates and then continues, "This is not in the original. There is an extra boat, tiny, right here, hardly noticeable amongst the sea until one looks closely."

"Okay," Lucy says while shrugging her shoulders, feeling a bit embarrassed for her husband's direct, loud, and drastic behavior.

"What about the boat?" Rachel inquisitively asks.

"First," Daryl comments, "it shouldn't be here. And secondly, it appears to have initials etched in it."

"What?" Rachel asks, concerned.

"Yes," Daryl claims. "Yes, and the boat, it is sinking into the water!"

Rachel gets up and walks over to the painting to investigate. After observing the painting over, she confirms, "You're right. There is another boat."

"I told you," Daryl states.

"And it's not in the original?" Rachel asks, feeling baffled.

"No."

"And," Rachel says, "it sure does look like there are," she suddenly pauses and then gasps, "Oh no!" as she recognizes the letters—"db." She slowly turns around, looking at Daryl as they both understand the possible implications.

Daryl says with deep concern, "I think we should not wait for Darren to return. I don't know what is happening, but we better go find him."

L INDA drives to 1355 Saint Street with Misty in the passenger seat and Eric and Cassie in the back seat. Eric lies resting with his head on Cassie's lap covered by a blanket for warmth. The ride is quiet because all are suspended in thought with mixed emotions in suspense for the unknown possibilities that may soon confront them. Linda stops at a four-way stop. She glances over at her mother, remembering when she was a kid walking with her parents and grandparents down this road after having dinner at her cousin's house many years ago. Swinging between the arms of her grandparents, she was happy and blissful. The memory is strong. Linda reaches over and gently places her right hand on her mother's forearm, offering a sign of affection during this unexpectedly joyful but mysterious time of their lives. There is an unusual feeling of closeness between them at this moment.

With no other cars around, Linda slowly pushes on the gas pedal, accelerating through the intersection. A few blocks down the road, they arrive at a small abandoned convenient store—1355 Saint Street. Linda turns into the cracked concrete and parks, waiting in silence. After a few minutes, a red Volkswagen pulls up next to them. A young man, in his mid-thirties, is wearing a red baseball cap and sunglasses. He slowly turns and faces them through the window, nodding and signaling them to follow him. They leave the parking lot.

The Volkswagen drives five miles per hour under the speed limit for about twenty-five minutes on the main street, winding like a long snake through the reservation. Then, slowing down, he veers off onto a gravel road for the next fifteen minutes, eventually turning down a long, twisting dirt road. Before following the car down the long road, Linda asks, "Well, we've gone this far, what do you all think? Do we continue?"

Misty replies, "Well, at this point, what do we have to lose?"

Linda follows the car down the road, reaching a single-wide, gray trailer. The Volkswagen drives around in a circle, not stopping, and passes them on the way out pointing at the trailer. Understanding the cue, Linda parks the car in front of the trailer.

"Cassie and Mom, wait here," Linda says before getting out. "Mom, get behind the wheel and let me go check this out for a minute. If anything seems strange, get the heck out of here."

"Darling," Misty says, "Haven't things been strange enough? We are here for a reason, so let's go in."

"Are you sure?"

"Yes," Misty responds, "I'm sure."

All of them get out of the car, with Eric hanging onto the shoulders of Cassie and Linda, as he is barely able to walk. Misty walks in front, reaching the front door. She pauses and then knocks. A man's high-pitched voice from inside yells, "Come in!"

Misty opens the door, and they all enter. Inside, they smell meat cooking. Linda closes the door behind them, and they stand looking at a slender man sitting on a white couch with neatly,-parted, short, gray hair. His piercing green eyes shine through a small pair of black-rimmed eyeglasses. He is wearing a red collared shirt with meticulously pressed tan dockers.

"Welcome," the man says. He points to the brown leather couch across from him and invites them over, "Please have a seat." They all walk to the couch and sit down. Being smooshed up tightly against each other, Eric rests his head on Cassie's shoulder.

Referring to Eric, the man asks, "How's he doing?"

Misty answers, "He will recover."

"Good," the man states, "What do you know about Eric?"

The women are not surprised that the man knows Eric's name, expecting this might be the man behind the "unknown number" phone calls; however, the voice from the phone calls was lower, but they are a bit taken back by the exact question.

"It depends on who you are asking," Linda replies, not willing to concede that this man might have the upper hand.

"Not really," the man states with certainty. "None of you, even you, Cassie, really know that much about him." All three ladies remain silent, waiting for further explanation. The man then continues, "Eric has something that we have been waiting for for a long time." He pauses and then says, "Eric, it is good to see you. We have been waiting for you."

Misty, Linda, and Cassie all look at each other after a few silent seconds pass by, wondering what this all means.

"Yes," the man says, "So, Eric, do you have it?"

Eric opens his eyes and with a struggle, softly says, "I don't know what you are talking about."

"Really?" The man expresses in disbelief. "You don't remember that you were given a blanket many years ago?"

Eric starts to think backwards in time for any hint of such memory, but his mental catalog is obscure. While Eric is trying to jumpstart his mind, a picture of his grandmother on her death bed suddenly flashes before him; then, another memory shoots across his mind, when he was twelve years old visiting his grandmother outside of Lima, Peru, while she was serving a Christian mission assisting the poor children with education. The memory plays out in his mind:

"My boy," she says to him, "Please come here."

Eric walks over and sits beside her on a flower-patterned couch in a small, rural, country house. The aroma of hand-made pan being made from her mission companions in the kitchen swarms throughout the place. The grandmother reaches into a hand-woven straw bag and pulls out a thin and faded white blanket. Handling it with reverence, she gently places it on her lap.

She quietly says, "My boy, this was given to me from my grandmother, who had it passed down to her from her grandmother, and so on. My plan was to continue the tradition in giving it to your sister, so she could pass it on to her grandchild, but I don't think I will be around her much longer."

Eric asks with concern, "What are you talking about?"

"My sensitive little boy," she says with a tender smile, "I am not feeling well."

"What do you mean?"

"Oh, that's my boy, got to understand."

"What's wrong?"

"I'm not feeling well, but more importantly, I keep getting a strong premonition that I won't be here much longer, and so I must give this to you, and you will know who to give it to when the time is right."

"But, grandma!" Eric cries with serious worry.

The ladies in the kitchen quiet.

"Now, my child, please listen," she says lovingly. "There will be people in the future who will come looking for this that want it for other things—you need to be careful and wise. You will learn this in the future. These people are bad people; they seem nice and kind, but they are ravening wolves inside. Do you understand what I am saying?"

Eric nods his head yes while continuing to feel confounded and sad that his grandmother is unwell.

"This might sound strange now," she states, "but this blanket contains truth that only the pure and honest of heart can see. Are you honest and pure of heart, my child?"

Eric pauses in order to respond truthfully, as she has taught him to be. "I don't know, grandma," he innocently responds.

"That's my honest boy. You will know if you are pure in heart when you are tested and tried with those things that are most precious to you." She pauses, winks, and then asks, "What is most precious to you?"

"I am not sure, probably my family and you."

"Grandson, you will be tested and tried, and when it comes knocking at your door remember our conversation here in the place with the lowly."

Eric, still innocent and young, is fully capable of comprehending the ideas of values and morals, understanding what she is saying.

"My grandson," she says with more seriousness to drive the point home, "This blanket is ancient and needs great care. You will know what to do with it at the right time, and follow that spiritual feeling that you have been taught."

The memory fades, and the man on the couch asks, "Eric, do you have it?"

With heavy and tired eyes, Eric gazes at the man with an intuitive feeling inside, not understanding why, that he must take this man to where the blanket is located. Eric replies softly, "Yes, I have it, but it is not here." He pauses, catching his breath, and continues, "I have kept in a safe place. I will take you there."

The man nods okay.

Darren's eyes pop open from napping on the bus. He reaches down for the sweater pocket wrapped underneath his arm to feel for the medallion placed inside. As his fingers slide over it, he offers a sigh of relief. He sits straight up and wonders where he is. The bus passes a highway destination sign: Montrose—ten miles. He thinks, Montrose? Did we already pass Grand Junction? I must have been asleep for a while. Then, a thought springs on him, Hey, isn't this where Daryl and Lucy are from? I think so. He pulls out his phone from his pant pocket to call Rachel and the battery has no charge. He puts his phone back into his pocket and scans out the window to the mountainous country scene, longing for his family back home.

Ten miles later the bus exits the highway and drives through town. It stops at a local gas station with people standing outside next to their luggage waiting to be picked-up. The driver announces, "Alright, everybody, we are here in Montrose and will have a fifteen-minute break. Be on the bus ready to go in fifteen minutes."

Darren puts on his sweater and walks off the bus, entering the gas station while following a fellow passenger into the restroom. As he waits his turn for an open stall, a six-foot and four-inch large, muscular man stands beside him. The man is wearing a black Colorado Rockies baseball cap, dark sunglasses, a denim long-sleeved collared shirt with jeans, and uniquely bright, shiny black sneakers. Darren starts feeling nervous because the man seems suspiciously dressed; and notices the man glancing at him from the corner of his eye.

The man suddenly asks Darren in friendliness, "Where are you headed?"

Uncertain of who this man is, Darren tersely replies, "South."

The man smiles and asks, "South, oh, where?"

Exactly at this moment, one of the stall doors opens becoming vacant. Being the next in line, Darren hurriedly says, "Gotta go!" He swiftly leaves and enters the stall, locking the door. He stands and waits, listening acutely for anything suspicious; however, all he hears is the sound of urinals and toilets flushing; stall doors opening, closing, and locking; and sink water running, washing hands. After a little while, the bathroom goes awkwardly quiet. Watching the floor outside the stall, Darren sees black shiny shoes walking towards him. Scared, he quickly turns and places the medallion behind the toilet, not visible from the front, and then flushes the toilet, acting as if he used it. He cautiously opens the door, and the man is standing, pointing a gun at him. The man demands, "Alright, you are going to give me what Robert gave you. I know you have it."

Darren, feeling terrified, stutters, "I d-d-don't know, wh-what you, you are, are talking about."

The man points the gun to Darren's forehead and angrily states, "Now, I know you know where it is! You have five seconds, and if you don't tell me, I will pull the trigger."

Darren's wife and kids flash before his eyes, and then he stutters, "O-o-okay, okay, d-d-don't sh-shoot!"

"Where is it?"

"O-okay. I, I will, ta-take you there."

"Where is it?"

"P-please, p-please, I have a family and I, I, know where it is, but, but pl-please I need to take you there," Darren stammers as sweat drips from his forehead.

"It can't be far!" The man yells.

"I have it, it's in my, my, bag, um, under the bus."

"Okay, retrieve your bag," the man orders, "and meet me behind the gas station in the alleyway."

"Yes, got, got it, got it."

PAUL MOSS

"Now," The man says, "You will walk in front of me. You try to run or tell someone, I shoot, and then I go after your family, got it?"

"O-o-okay, got it, got, got it."

Darren, trying to calm his nerves, swiftly walks out of the stall toward the restroom door with the man following closely behind. They reach the door, and the man says, "Unlock it." Darren unlocks the door, and they exit the restroom and station. Outside, people are entering the bus getting ready to leave. Finding the bus driver standing next to the bus, Darren asks, "Hey, I'm going to be getting off here. Can I get my bag underneath the bus?"

The bus driver asks with agitation, "What do you mean? You didn't say anything about this before you left the bus. Is this your final destination?"

Darren says, "Yeah, sorry."

The bus driver gazes at him in doubt, noticing Darren's heavy perspiration on his forehead and heavier breathing, as if scared. The driver shakes his head and says, "Hey, man, are you okay? If you are not, you better let me know, hear me, young man?"

Darren shakes his head and says, "Everything is okay, sir. I just need my bag and we are all good. I'm okay."

The bus driver puts his cigarette out and walks over to where the passengers' bags are kept below. Darren follows him, and the driver retrieves the backpack and, while handing it to Darren, he asks again, "Hey, man, are you sure that you are okay?"

Darren looks the bus driver right in the eyes and lies, "Yes, sir."

The bus driver shakes his head in disbelief and says, "Hey, man, you better watch out for yourself. This world is a no-good, dirty, dangerous place."

Darren nods and says, "Thank you, sir." Taking his backpack, he turns around and heads to the side of the gas station where the man is watching him. Darren turns the corner of the building, and the man follows him to the back alleyway. They stop, and Darren says with conviction, "It is here in my backpack, but let me get to your car and I will give it to you then."

"Give it to me now." the man demands, taking a step closer to Darren.

Hearing the bus leave the station, and while bending down holding his backpack in his right hand, Darren, surprisingly, with force, slings the backpack at the man, hitting him off-balance, allowing for a few fleeting moments. Darren turns and runs, swerving around a black dumpster. *Ding*, a bullet ricochets from the metal. He runs across the street and *zoom*, another bullet rushes by him. Turning down a nearby street of homes, *zoom*, another bullet hits a tree trunk. Sprinting past the first house, he takes a sharp turn to the backyard, jumping over a tall fence—his adrenaline is pouring into his veins.

Continuing to hurdle one fence after another and dashing across streets, Darren stops at an old red-brick home with broken windows covered in vines, appearing vacant. His blood is pumping intensely as he listens to all the sounds around him with his eyes rapidly moving back and forth like windshield wipers vigorously working to keep the pouring rain off the front glass. Cautiously stepping to the front of the house, he slowly pokes his head forward around the corner, surveying the unkempt front yard and street ahead. He hears a car coming down the street, so he quickly runs back behind the house, hiding.

The car moves at a slow pace like a slug in the night ready to consume fresh leaves from any nearby edible plant. Darren pokes his head again around the corner, watching a black-windowed car drive up and stop. "It's got to be them," Darren says to himself as sweat runs down over his lips. The car's back door opens, and a tall, thin man with a long jawline and sunken eyes steps out wearing a black, cotton, rimmed hat, light green jacket, and a white collared shirt with tan pants. He pans the area and then looks straight ahead, walking forward. Before stepping up the street curb and onto the sidewalk, he pauses, continuing to keenly watch the premises with both hands remaining in his jacket pockets. Suddenly, his head turns, looking up the street as a group of kids come around the corner, walking toward him. The man stops and turns back around, walking back to the car. He gets inside the car, and it drives off.

Darren wipes his profusely sweating forehead and breathes a sigh of relief. Now, sitting down behind the house, he hears the kids laughing and giggling as they pass by. Oh, thank you kids, Darren thinks in exhausted gratitude. Not wanting to wait and see if the car is to return, he decides he better keep moving. He rises from the ground and peeks around the house once more, watching and listening for anything peculiar. As the scene appears clear, Darren dashes from behind the house and sprints behind houses and jumps over fences, moving like a freight train fueled by a survival motor engine.

While steaming ahead, Darren abruptly notices that he can't hear anything; everything is silent—there is no sound to his steps as his feet touch the ground nor noise to his hands as the fingers grab the wooden fences, nor whistling wind over his sweater as he runs. He takes his finger and pinches himself to affirm that he is, yet, still able to feel. Pain sharply reaches his muscles, so he deaccelerates, concerned about his health, wondering if it might be early signs of a heart attack, stroke, or possible heat exhaustion. He thinks, I haven't been running that long, maybe twenty minutes, but no longer than a half-hour. He looks up to the passing blue sky and sees an eagle soaring high above him. Instantaneously, like turning on car speakers full blast, his ears are overwhelmed with the eagle's piercing scream, penetrating throughout his entire body with an electric vibration. This surge to his senses stales his movement to thwarted stillness. However, desiring for further safety away from whomever is attempting to take the medallion, he tries to take one more step forward. With all his strength, he barely raises his foot into the air, and as he moves it downward, he glances at the ground beneath him, and the earth is rapidly appearing to melt, thus suspending his step in mid-air, standing motionless as a two-thousand-year-old Greek marble statue. Not knowing why a swift sensational tingling feeling moves throughout his entire body, he wonders if he's starting to hallucinate due to fatigue or other bodily malfunctions. However, instantly, without warning, his body begins to regain its normalcy with a lowering rhythmic heartbeat in his chest, calmer breathing, and soothing emotions. Darren gazes up to the sky and does not see the eagle flying above. Strange, Darren thinks. Feeling uncertain if he should place his foot on the ground again, in fear that some strange and unforeseeable event may suddenly take place, he decides to push onward and give it another try. He gradually moves his foot to the earth, and as it touches solid matter, he says to himself, "Touchdown." With reality tested and assured, he begins to move forward, running.

Knowing that he should soon communicate for help, and also call home, so that Rachel is not totally worried, he begins to think where he might be able to use a phone. He passes by a dark-blue-and green-trimmed two-story house with a covered front porch. Inside, Darren thinks, someone's got to have a phone that I can use. Carefully walking up the first two steps of the house, he scans the premises for any inconsistent nuance that might scare him away. Everything seems okay, so he moves over the last step and onto the porch. As he moves toward the door, he glances into the window investigating if anyone is inside—he hears a car coming down the street. Without a second thought while continuing in such highly uncharacteristic behavior as he reacts in survival mode, Darren reaches for the doorknob, turns it to the right, and enters the home, quickly shutting the door behind him.

"He's not answering," says Rachel desperately with sadness as she sits in one of the two middle cargo seats in the Token's white van while driving on the freeway to find Darren. Daryl is steering and Lucy is beside him in the front passenger seat; John is in the other cargo seat next to his mother, and Roger and Stephanie are in the back. Glancing through the rearview mirror, Daryl curls his lips in disappointment to the news. Lucy glances back at Rachel, shaking her head without words to express. John says with confidence, "Mom, everything will be okay." Rachel shrugs her shoulders, hoping that John is right. She lays the cell phone down on her lap, anxiously waiting for Darren to call back. The unknowns to Darren's status are beginning to swarm her thoughts with worry. A memory begins to arise within her mind of when Darren made a peculiar comment to her a long time ago, which imprinted itself firmly on the pages of her pure soul:

John was born two months prematurely. Rachel and Darren were in the hospital watching their son struggle to stay alive through a glass infant incubator. With uncanniness, Darren whispered to her a reverent and tonal-shaped comment that embarked a twisting prism from the physical world to the eternal realms beyond: "Sweetheart, our family will be forever." As these words entered her eardrums, a strikingly warm sensation zipped from the top of her head down to the bottom of her feet, leaving her in a moment of awe. Her mental horizon shifted from a picture consisting merely of earthly, nuclear familial meals inside a modest home with laughter and smiles to a heavenly and celestial space that was beautifully yoked with a glorious, gemmed, and crystal-clear round table providing enough seats and food for all human families in existence—before, now, and in the future—to a never-ending peaceful, relational enjoyment, bound by some alchemist agent, securing loved ones with the glorious reality to remain together forever without the decaying destiny of death's holding grip.

After all these years, this simple moment and thought-provoking phrase by her husband still burns a flame bright with hope for a better world—a more complete and inclusive joining of peoples. This feeling coupled with Darren's unresponsiveness creates a swelling of emotions within her, and however close her bursting feelings are to her skin's surface, her tough inner strength chokes them down in order to prevent an emotional breakdown in front of her kids.

Daryl begins to slow the vehicle down and pulls over to the freeway's shoulder, stopping twenty yards behind a car with its hazards blinking. Lucy sternly asks, "What are you doing? You know we don't have time for this."

"We all need a bit of a breather," Daryl replies, "It will be good to get some fresh air."

Lucy rolls her eyes in disgust with Daryl's timing to stop in such a stressful situation for Rachel and the kids. "Wait here. Let me check it out," he says before opening the door. He exits the van and walks toward the car. He stops at the rear tinted window, striving to look through it, but can't, so he proceeds to the back door. As he reaches the door, the window gradually rolls down and the barrel of a shotgun points at him.

"Get in the car!" a raspy voice commands.

Stunned, Daryl initially remains still. He looks back at Lucy and the man in the car explicitly says, "Hey, don't think about it! I'll shoot!" Daryl shakes his head, no, as if to say, Lucy, don't you dare get out of the car. "Gosh darnit!" The man yells. "I told you not to try any funny business!" Daryl has a small smirk without any fear. The man demands, "Get in here, now!" The door opens and Daryl enters the car.

Daryl sits next to the man with the shotgun. He is stocky with round cheeks, a small forehead, and wide nose. Sitting in the front passenger seat and facing forward is an older man wearing a white cowboy hat. Daryl cannot see the driver, but notices that he is wearing black gloves. The old man in the front calmly states, "We don't have time. Let's get going." They drive off.

Screeccchhhhhhhh, the Tokens' white van goes speeding forwards, following the car. Rachel has hopped from the back to the front seat and is driving. Lucy and the kids have ducked down below for safety.

WITH his back pressed against the front door, Darren stands inside the house. His eyes frantically scan what is in front of him: to the right is a living room and straight ahead is a narrow hallway leading to a kitchen. The place is quiet. Carefully tiptoeing down the hallway, he slides against the wall, stopping at the kitchen's entrance. He waits to hear for any voices or noises. As it remains soundless, he pokes his head around the corner, watching in both directions. There is another hallway leaving the kitchen with two doors in it. There is a back door that goes outside to the backyard. Darren carefully enters three steps into the kitchen and the wood floor squeaks. From one of the rooms down the hallway, a young boy's voice yells, "Mom, is that you?" In a split second, Darren rushes toward the back door, hoping to slip out and avoid being caught. As he reaches for the doorknob and turns the handle—it squeaks—it's jammed. "Mom, are you home from shopping?" the boy's voice yells as Darren now hears tiny footsteps coming down the hallway. Darren goes into panic mode and furiously shakes the doorhandle, trying to pry it open, but the door still will not open. Hastily gazing around for somewhere to hide, he is trapped and turns his head around to see who is coming. A small, nine-year-old boy with blonde hair and green hazel eyes, enters the kitchen looking at him. Darren looks down at the boy and the boy peacefully says, "I knew you were coming here."

Darren's astounded.

"I saw you in a dream," the boy says.

Darren instantaneously hears an eagle chirp loudly in his ears. The boy takes a few steps towards Darren and stops right in front of him, staring up at him. The boy says confidently, "It is time."

Darren, feeling a bit hazy between the real and fictitious, blinks his eyes a few times and then opens them wide open—the boy is gone. What? he thinks. What the heck is going on with me? Something is not right. Now, with his back pressed up against the back door, feeling a bit unnerved, as if he is losing his mind, he continues thinking, It seemed so real. He hears a car pull up in front of the house. He quickly turns around and turns the doorknob—this time it opens freely. He leaves the house, running to the backyard fence, and is about to jump over when he hears a guy yelling from the front of the house, "Hurry, we need to get back, we have them!" Darren pauses. The car pulls around the corner and he hides below the wooden fence. Through a small opening in the fence, he watches the car that was following him drive by.

What now? Darren thinks. Knowing that he needs to act, he runs back into the house where he exited, rushing through it in search for a phone. Finally finding one in an empty bedroom, Darren dials Rachel's phone number.

"Hello," Rachel answers.

"Rachel," Darren quietly says.

"Sweetheart!" Rachel exclaims. "Oh, so good to hear your voice! I was getting so worried about you!"

"Oh, my love," Darren states, out of breath, "So good to hear your voice, too. Are you okay?"

"Well, not exactly," she says. "Someone has Daryl."

"Someone, what, has got him?" Darren asks, not understanding.

"Yes, some people by the side of the road just picked him up and took off."

"Oh my gosh. Is he okay?"

"I hope so," Rachel states. "We are following them right now."

"And the kids? Lucy?"

"They are fine," she says. "We are all together."

"Good." Darren says and continues, "Where are you guys?"

"We were on our way to find you."

"Really?" he asks with surprise. "Why?"

"We felt we needed to."

"Strange," Darren comments, "We don't have much time to discuss things. Where are you guys?"

"We are passing Rifle, Colorado."

"I'm in Montrose." Darren states.

"Really?" Rachel asks with excitement.

"Yes."

"Wow, we are close."

"Wow is right," Darren confirms. "I will wait for you guys to get here."

"Sounds good."

"You need to be very careful," Darren says, "It looks like there are people hunting us down—they are not good people. They are looking for something, but not sure exactly what for." He pauses and continues, "Oh, shoot, someone is coming, got to run. I will call you in a while. Love ya."

"Darren, wait, are you okay?" Rachel hurriedly asks, not wanting to stop hearing his voice.

The phone hangs up.

A green minivan pulls up to the gray single-wide trailer in the Hopi reservation. Inside the trailer, the man with the high-pitched voice says to Eric, "Okay, where are we going?"

Eric tries to sit up and move his head from Cassie's shoulder, but still does not have the strength to manage it. Out of the corner of his mouth, he whispers, "It is here on the rez."

"What?" the man, in unbelief, asks.

"Yes," Eric clearly confirms.

"You will take us there?"

"Yes."

"Okay," the man says and stands up from the couch, walking to the front door.

Misty and Linda stand up and help Cassie raise Eric to his feet. With the man in front, they all leave the trailer and enter the minivan.

"Okay, where are we going?" the man asks Eric.

"The old farmhouse, Deborah and Rusty Walk-the-Horse's old place," Eric tiredly says.

The man glances at the driver, who is wearing sunglasses and a faded yellow ball cap with a black t-shirt and blue jeans, and asks him, "Do you know where this is?"

"Yes," the driver responds.

"How long?"

"Fifteen to twenty minutes away."

"Good."

On the drive, Eric rests while Cassie stares out the window, not knowing where she is; Misty and Linda sit in the back seat watching all the memory-filled surroundings. The minivan eventually rides up to an abandoned log home that has only half a roof, one window, and no front door—the old farmhouse.

The man asks Eric, "Is this the place?"

"Yes," Eric responds with more vigor, as his strength is gaining.

The driver parks in front of the farmhouse. They all exit the van, with Linda being the last one to leave. As she is about to get out of the vehicle, she looks back at the young driver—he is staring right at her through the sunglasses. There is something about his face that seems noticeable to her. Not having much time, Linda steps out of the van and closes the door behind her.

Eric wraps his arms through and around Cassie's and Linda's arms to secure his balance. "Eric, are you sure that it is here?" Cassie whispers.

He shakes his head yes to conserve energy, saying, "Behind the house."

"Alright, where is it?" the man asks, impatiently.

Eric and the ladies begin walking around to the back of the old house as the man follows them. "Keep going," Eric whispers to the ladies, "Another fifty steps towards that small tree." As they walk, Eric quietly counts, "forty-seven, forty-eight, forty-nine, fifty," and he stops. "It is here. Buried right here."

Cassie thinks, How in the world could anything be buried here; Eric has never mentioned this place to me before. How does Eric know this place?

Linda smiles and asks quietly, "Right here, Eric?"

Eric shakes his head up and down. Linda yells, "It is right here!"

The man walking behind them yells, "Right there?"

Linda yells, "Yes!"

The man walks up to and stands beside Linda, asking, "It is right here? I don't see anything."

"It is buried," Linda states.

"Buried right here underneath the ground?" The man asks doubtingly.

Eric nods his head yes.

"How far down?" the man demands.

Eric quietly says while being out of breath, "Two to three feet."

"We have a shovel in the back of the minivan," the man says, "I'll go get it."

After collecting the shovel, the man returns and starts digging. After five minutes in what is relatively sandy loam soil, the shovel hits an object, making a *clink* sound. "I think we've hit something," the man says with excitement. He then asks Eric, "Is it in some kind of a metal box?"

Eric nods yes. The man digs around the box, uncovering it. It is a welded steel box with a top and rusted lock. He reaches down and lifts the box out of the hole, placing it up on the ground. Eric and the ladies stand looking down at it. The man steps up out of the hole and begins to strike the lock with the shovel multiple times—it does not break. Eric offers a small, prideful grin. After trying it a few more times without prevail, the man gasps while asking, "How do we open it? Is there a key?"

Eric replies, "I don't have the-," he pauses to catch his breath, "key."

"We will break it open, then," the man demands. "Let's go back to the trailer."

The man bends down, picks up the box with both hands, and starts walking back to the van. Eric stands, staring out at the desert landscape scenery ahead with emotions swelling with deep sentiment. As he looks out over the hill a thousand yards away, Eric states with reverence, "This place was special to me."

The man yells, "Are you guys coming?" as he continues walking forward.

"We better get going," remarks Linda.

"Thanks for taking a second," Eric says to the ladies.

As they are about to turn and leave, they notice two large and majestic bull elk appear on the hillside peak—standing erect and alert, peering down at them. Sensing that the elk are focused on something beyond the group, they turn around to see if there is anything nearby. The only thing visible to them is the back of the man who is walking away. As they turn back around, the elk instantaneously bolt down the hillside, running through bushes and trees with intense fury and purpose—stunning is the burst of speed these athletically graceful and powerful animals are—sparking awe-filled wonder at nature's creations. The man shouts, "Hurry, let's get going, hurry up!" The elk pick up speed, now seeming like they are floating through the air, covering tremendous amounts of ground between each bounce.

The man holding the box stops and turns back around, only to see the others standing and gazing forward in the same spot where he saw them last. As he opens his mouth, about to yell at them to start moving, his foot hits a rock, making him stumble and fall. The box slips from his hands and slams onto the ground, breaking the lock open. The man smiles because he feels luck is on his side. As he begins to rise from the ground, he hears a unique pounding sound coming from behind. Unsure about this sensation, he looks back at the others—they are still motionless, appearing like frozen statues. His eyes quickly grab hold of the two fast-moving elk that are pouncing toward him. The elk are breathing heavily and snorting furiously as they first approach the four others. The group all stand closely together, holding each other tightly, turning their heads slightly at an angle downward preparing for a head on collision. The elk dash right past them, moving toward the man. The man scurries backwards with his arms and legs skidding on the dirt, and then, while raising both of his arms up for protection from the anticipated crash, he closes his eyes, ready for impact, but feels nothing more than a breeze of wind rush over and past him. He opens his eyes, and watches Misty pick up the metal box from the ground, holding it in her arms in front of him.

The man then glances around, wondering where the elk ran off to—they disappeared with no trace, not even footprints. The man attempts to raise himself from the ground, but cannot move his lower body. Suddenly, blood runs from his nose and he begins coughing. His lungs panic, gasping for air, but no air molecules enter. He viciously grips both hands around his throat and begins to shake feverishly. Rolling his upper body over to the side, he lies motionless with his chest and face in the dirt—dead.

Misty quickly yells to the others, "Let's get out of here!"

As they are all about to leave, the driver of the minivan stands at the side of the house, staring at them. All four look at him, feeling unsure of who this young man is and what he is about to do. Through his sunglasses, the young man's face is pointed directly at Linda for a few brief moments. Then he glances at the box in Misty's hand, then down at the dead man. He leisurely walks toward them and asks Misty, "What happened to him?"

Misty directly responds, "He died."

"How?"

"I don't really know," she replies, "It seems as though he had a stroke of some kind."

The young man then looks at Linda. He then takes a few steps forward while removing his ball cap and sunglasses. His long, black hair falls down to the middle of his back. Reaching Linda, he stops, stares deeply into her eyes, and poignantly asks her, "Do you recognize me?"

Linda stands, pondering his facial features, yes, recognizing him, but unsure if it is really who she thinks it is.

"Mom," he then says to her.

"Can it be?" she asks with tremendous shock.

"Yes, Mom, it is me, Joseph."

Linda inherently steps forward toward him, astounded with doubt as her hands lift upward to touch his smooth and chubby cheeks. She moves her fingers to his lips, then forehead, and back down to his cheeks, pressing them to make sure he is real, not sure what to feel.

"Mom, it's me, Joseph, your boy."

Her fingers slide down from his face to wrapping her arms around him, holding him tightly and gently like a precious doll.

"Is it really you?" whispers Linda in his ear.

"Yes, Mom, Joseph."

Linda beings to weep for joy, and the longing to see her son after so many years vanishes.

"I truly can't believe it," she remarks, astonished.

Joseph embraces her warmly.

Misty places the box onto the ground and like a magnet gravitates to the emotional scene she is witnessing. While looking at Joseph, she is in amazement, for it has been many years since she has seen both Linda and now her grandson. Joseph and Linda stop embracing and turn to Misty. Misty says with tender emotion, "Is it you, Joseph, my beautiful grandson? Oh, how beautiful this is."

Joseph nods his head yes and then calmly says, "Grandma, it is wonderful to see you."

Misty embraces him. The tears pour like Niagara Falls from her eyes. Once Misty and Joseph stop embracing, Linda asks, "My son, what are you doing here?"

"Mom," Joseph says, "I would love to tell you, but I don't think we have time right now. We better get going." He pauses, glancing at the box on the ground, and says, "Let's take that and your friends—I know of a small cave about two thousand yards from here up in the mountains where I think we'll be safe." He turns around, making sure nobody is behind them, and then continues, "There will be more people coming here. If we disappear for a while, they may search for us somewhere else, and then we can plan from there."

"Where is the cave up the mountain?" Linda asks.

"Do you see that hill up to the south?"

"Yes," she replies.

"It is just past it. A perfect little spot to hide out for a couple of hours or more, if we need to." Seeing Eric draped over Cassie, Joseph asks his mom, "Do you think he can make it?"

Linda responds, "I think so."

Misty asks Joseph, "Is there fresh water up there?"

"Yes, we can get some."

"Okay, let's get going," Misty states, affirmatively.

Joseph walks directly up to Cassie and Eric and kindly says, "Let me take him from here." Joseph then slides his shoulder underneath Eric's armpit, supporting his weight. Linda goes over and picks up the metal box. They all start moving for the cave.

"Hello," Rachel answers her phone while still driving the Token's white van, following the black car that has Daryl.

"Rach, it's me, Darren."

"Oh, sweetheart, I'm so glad to hear your voice!"

"You, too."

"Why do you keep calling me from random numbers?"

"My cell phone is dead, and I'm calling from a convenience store."

"What happened?"

"I'll tell you later. Are you still following that car with Daryl?"

"Yes."

"Have you tried calling for help, 911?"

"Yes, we've called 911," she states, "and told them about what happened and said that they will have somebody call us back, but we haven't heard anything since we started following them."

"That's not surprising."

"Really?"

"Our phones are probably tapped," he says, "so any outgoing or incoming calls, texts, can be intercepted."

"How?"

"Not sure, but they are probably listening to our conversation right now."

"What should we do?"

"Keep going—how far are you from Montrose?"

"Ten minutes."

Darren hesitates and then says with apprehension, "We will have to find Daryl another way."

"Are you sure?"

"Yes, my suspicion is that they are after me. We will find him later."

"Why?"

"Because I believe I have something of theirs."

"What?" Rachel asks with surprise.

"I'll explain later," Darren pauses and continues, "tell Lucy that he will be fine."

"I'll try."

"Okay," he says, "This might be the only chance to get me, and who knows where that car will go with Daryl."

"True," Rachel states clearly, "It might be best if you talk to Lucy."

"There isn't time."

"Okay."

"There will be a small underpass that you will go through when you come into Montrose. I will be there on the right side wearing what I wore when I left Denver. I'll be showing the gift that you gave me at the station. Now, only slow down, but don't stop all the way when you pick me up. I'll jump in the vehicle, and we will go from there," he pauses and then continues, "Does that sound okay?"

"Okay," she confirms with serious emotional conflict: on the one hand, feeling tremendously excited to see her husband and have him safely near, but deeply troubled for Daryl and Lucy's situation and how difficult it will be to tell her the plan.

"Got to run. I'll see you there."

"Love ya," she says.

"Love you, too."

Rachel hangs up the phone, not really knowing what to say next to Lucy. She places the phone in the middle console.

Lucy asks, "What did he say?"

"He is in Montrose, and we are going to pick him up. Also, he thinks these people are after him—he has something of theirs."

"What?" Lucy asks, knowing that this might be what is needed to get her husband back.

"He didn't say."

"Didn't say?" Lucy asks excitedly, "Why not?"

Rachel softly answers because she knows that what she is about to say is mostly selfish, "He said there wasn't time."

"Why doesn't he give it back to these guys, so we can get Daryl back and be on our way home?" Lucy now asks with angst.

"I don't know, but he did say that he thinks Daryl will be fine."

"Daryl is not fine!"

"I know," Rachel agrees, accompanied by a long silence. With no words to sufficiently appease the situation, Rachel decides to blurt it out: "Darren said that we will have to find Daryl another way."

"What?" Lucy asks with surprise to what seems to her as logical absurdity.

"Look," Rachel says, "We don't know where this car is going, and we have a chance to pick up Darren—should we not take it?"

"And Daryl?"

Rachel reassures her, "I know this sounds all wild, I know. Darren is confident that they are after him, and Daryl will be okay."

"This is all too crazy!" Lucy exclaims, flustered, while turning and looking out the window.

"Yes, it is!" Rachel states, hoping that Lucy will understand.

Lucy thinks of her husband in this awful and seemingly dangerous circumstance. She can't bear the thought of losing him. He has been a rock of stability to her and their family. She begins to cry, feeling sad and exhausted by all this. Solemnly, through her tears, she states, "This just doesn't make any sense. Why all the trouble? First, we are in the hunt for your lost husband, and now we luckily find him, and now I'm losing mine."

Rachel reaches over and places her hand over Lucy's hand, offering a physical touch of empathy. Lucy places her hand on top of Rachel's, and, while glancing at her, unselfishly states, "Daryl and I were a part of this from the beginning, so we will see it to the end—let's hope Darren is right."

"I'm sorry," Rachel sincerely expresses.

"Daryl is a big boy," Lucy says, being positive. "He can take care of himself. So, what's the plan?"

"We are going to go into town and pick up Darren underneath the underpass."

"Alright."

Rachel grabs onto the steering wheel with both hands and mentally focuses on executing the plan with precision. They reach the exit and start veering off the highway. Lucy watches the car with Daryl inside as it continues to drive straight ahead. As the two cars drift apart from each other, she can't help but feel Daryl's absence increase and her worry intensify. There was a sense of comfort knowing that he was in that car in front, even if she didn't know if he was okay or not. She inherently shakes her head, feeling more sad and deeply troubled.

Coming to a stop at the exit, Rachel turns right. After going a quarter of a mile, they begin to approach the underpass, and in front of it stands a man wearing large sunglasses looking down, hiding much of his face, and a short-sleeved blue shirt with denim jeans, just as Darren was wearing when he left Denver, except for the large sunglasses, and there is no sweater. Rachel's instincts tell her to be cautious.

"Is this Darren?" Lucy asks.

"Not exactly sure," Rachel responds, watching for the bracelet to be shown as a sign.

As they approach the man, Rachel swerves the car over to the right of the lane, slowing down. Immediately ahead, another man comes running towards them from the other side of the underpass, waving his arms in the air, with a gray sweater in one hand. Rachel and Lucy's attention move to this man.

Lucy asks, "Is that Darren?"

"I'm not sure."

Rachel slows down even more, and the cars behind her start to honk. The man they are approaching keeps his head pointed to the ground without showing his face. As they drive closer, the man slightly raises his head showing his chin and mouth. Rachel then glances back at the man who is running at them and sees what looks like the bracelet she gave Darren at the station on his wrist, she immediately yells, "This is not him!" Rachel quickly pushes on the accelerator, driving past the first man and onto the second. Approaching the other man with his arms still waving, Rachel shouts, "This is him!"

Rachel slows down and the sliding door opens. Darren jumps into the van yelling, "Hurry! Push on it!" The other man sprints after them, being only thirty feet away. With the van door not shut, Rachel steps on the gas, swerving into the lane. The momentum of the van thrusts the door forward, missing Darren's leg by inches. They drive away up the street.

Once up the hill, Darren says excitingly to his children, "Hey kiddos, great to see you!" The kids smile, and Johnny, who is sitting in the other cargo seat without his seatbelt fastened, cries, "Daddy, daddy, we missed you!"

"Oh, my kids, how I've missed you!" Darren notices that Johnny does not have his seatbelt attached and asks, "Was that you who opened up the door?"

"Yeah," he says with enthusiasm.

"That's my boy!"

Rachel shouts, "I think we might have some trouble!"

"What do you mean?" Darren asks.

"That guy," Rachel says, "underneath the underpass running after us. I saw him get into a car, and they are following us."

Lucy, knowing the area from her high school days, gives direction, "Okay, take this next left."

They turn left. The street is straight and then bends to the left. As they go around the bend, Darren looks back and sees the car that was chasing him. He shouts, "That is the same car!"

Lucy says to Rachel, "This road will come to a *T*, then take another left. If my memory is right, it will take us back to the main road."

"Then what?" Rachel asks.

Darren asks Lucy, "Do you think it is smart to stick around here?"

Lucy has no remaining family members living in the area. They all moved away a few years ago. "I don't know anyone here anymore," she states.

"Do you remember where the sheriff's station is in town?"

"Yes, it is across town."

Something inside Darren tells him to get back on the highway. He argues with the feeling, thinking, Why? He thinks going to the sheriff's station may be the best bet to get help. Robert's face on the bus flashes into his mind, and he remembers him saying, "Keep this safe." Darren reaches down over his pant pocket and feels the medallion inside it. Before going to the underpass to meet the others, he went back to the convenience store where he hid the medallion in the stall and retrieved it.

Darren has a thought and asks Rachel, "How much gas do we have?"

"A little more than three-quarters of a tank."

"Let's get back on the freeway," Darren says, knowing it does not make much logical sense.

"Why not go to the sheriff's?" asks Rachel, not understanding Darren's thinking.

"Because the police might be involved."

"Really?"

"Maybe," Darren states. "Something is telling me we should get out of here and head back south on the highway. It does not sound too logical, but has anything been too logical lately?"

Both Rachel and Lucy nod, agreeing with him. They turn left at the T and it winds them back to the main street and highway entrance. They enter the highway, and the car that was following them is a few cars behind.

E   RIC takes a long breath and tiredly steps up the hillside,
        but he is feeling a little better. His right arm is wrapped
        over Joseph's neck and shoulders. Misty, Linda, and
Cassie are a few feet behind them. Coming to a big boulder, the
young men slide past it, inching their way forward. As they move
around the boulder, they stop, looking at a short, elderly Native
American man who is standing in front of them with long braided
hair dressed in a casual blue t-shirt and blue jeans.

The elderly man says to the young men, "We have been
waiting for you to come." The man steps forward, placing his
arm underneath Eric's armpit to assist with the weighty load of
his sluggish body. The ladies pass around the boulder, with their
eyes expanding in amazement as they see the newly appearing
man underneath's Eric arm. The man looks back at them, saying,
"Hurry." There is a peaceful assurance accompanying his voice and
demeanor, somewhat recognizable. After walking another fifty
feet, the elderly man points further up the hill to a protruding rock
shaped like a bird's beak and says, "There."

Arriving at the rock, they all maneuver around it. In the
crevice, where the rock pushes itself out, lays a mangled mess of
large pine needle limbs covering a four-foot cave opening. The
elderly man removes the debris and points to the cave's entrance
for the others to enter. After they all slide in, the man, from the
inside, places the limbs back on the opening to cover it. The cave
is pitch black with a small light flickering in the distance showing
a dim path ahead. The cave ceiling stands four-feet tall and is an
arm-length's width.

"Follow the light," the man's voice commands through the
musty, cool, dense air. Following the wavy light, they reach a large

candle that is placed in a black metal base on the floor. Next to the candle, coming up through the thick granite floor, is a wooden ladder. The man motions them to go down. Joseph goes down the ladder first, then Eric, Cassie, Linda, Misty, and lastly the elderly man. At the bottom of the ladder is a small, candle-lit room with a winding, lighted corridor leaving it. As the man steps down from the ladder, he points to the corridor, stating, "Down there." After moving around a few bends, they arrive and stop at a loosely hanging elk skin covering with a white circular design painted on it, which is attached to the ceiling, acting as a curtain. The elderly man says, "Go ahead, it's okay." As they walk through the covering, it opens to a large, circlular, warm room, lit from a compact fire inside a small, stone pit. The walls are painted with various animals and plant species, along with a variety of circular designs in red and black pigment. There are two wooden benches sitting against the wall. At the other end of the room hangs another elk skin covering.

The elderly man walks around the others and helps Joseph gently lay Eric by the fire to absorb its heat. The man motions Cassie to sit down beside him. Joseph, Linda, and Misty remain standing a few feet behind Joseph and Cassie. The elderly man then leaves through the other elk skin covering and returns with three rugs in hand as others enter the room behind him. The man walks toward the fire as the other people stand, circling the room. He places one rug underneath Eric and Cassie and then the other next to them for the others to sit on. He walks to the other side of the fire and then places the other rug onto the ground. He motions at Linda to offer him the metal box that she still holds in her hands. Linda glances at her mother for confirmation that it is okay, and Misty nods up and down. Linda walks over to the man and gently hands him the box.

The elderly man bends down to the ground, placing the box down onto the rug. He stands and steps away. An elderly woman from the onlookers walks over to the box, kneels down beside it, and opens it. With both hands, she reaches in and pulls out the faded white blanket that was given to Eric by his grandmother. The blanket is worn and thin. It has red, white, blue, and black stars throughout. In the middle is a large woven hummingbird with the most exquisite and detailed workmanship. There is a small circular hole in the hummingbird's eye at the blanket's center.

Draped over her aged hands, the elderly woman takes the blanket and slowly moves around the fire toward Eric. The woman gently places the blanket over him and begins to sing a prayer. Eric's breathing immediately slows, and his eyes begin to soften inside his shut eyelids. After a few moments, he begins to moan as if in a tense dream. The lady stops singing. Eric opens his eyes and gazes into the fire's light, thinking upon his sudden vision. He sits up with the blanket flowing over his body and glances at Cassie, grinning, as if seeming to comprehend something new, bringing him joy. The lady slowly removes the blanket. Eric reaches over and embraces Cassie and whispers, "I feel so good. I haven't felt this good in so long. It is time to reunite with my parents."

The elderly woman hands the blanket to two other women that leave with it through the elk covering at the other side of the room, from where they came in. Standing on the other side of the fire, the elderly man asks Eric, "Are you ready to go heal others?"

Eric nods yes with a bright smile.

The man then turns to Misty, Linda, and Joseph and asks, "Would you like to come with us?"

Misty humbly replies, "Yes."

The onlookers around the room begin to leave through the elk covering from where they entered. The elderly man points for Misty, Linda, and Joseph to follow them. As the three reach the elk covering, Misty turns around and says to Eric and Cassie, "You'll be fine. We must go with our people." They leave the room.

The elderly man, Eric, and Cassie are left alone in the room. The man says, "It is time you go find your mom and dad." The man motions for Eric and Cassie to stand up, and then he escorts them out the cave. Outside the cave, the elderly man instructs, "Now, go, follow your heart, it will lead you to them." The elderly man reenters the cave.

"Do you have a map here in the van?" Darren asks Lucy as they travel south on the highway.

"Yeah," Lucy states as she reaches underneath her seat and pulls out a map, handing it to him.

Darren opens the map, commenting, "Let's see where we are." He then thinks, Where do we need to go? The conversation with Robert on the bus pops into his mind again—the Grand Canyon. "Alright," Darren says, "this is going to keep sounding a bit crazy, but I think we need to go to Arizona."

"Arizona?" Rachel questions, not believing her ears.

"Yes, I know, it is crazy," he states, "but I think we should keep moving on and connect some dots."

"What dots?"

"I ran into a guy on the bus, and he was going to the Grand Canyon. Ever since I met this man, my life has been wild."

"Before then!" Rachel corrects him.

"Well, yeah, of course," Darren agrees, "Things have not exactly been normal, but since meeting this man on the bus, things have gone absolutely crazy—we are being hunted, and Daryl is kidnapped. I believe we need to go to Arizona and find where this man is from and find some of his family. They might have some answers."

"Do you even know this man's name?" asks Rachel with impatience and continued doubt of Darren's thinking.

"Robert Hanson."

"Strange," Lucy interjects, "I had a dream last night and the man in the dream said his name was Robert, and he was-" she suddenly pauses.

"Uh-huh?" Darren eagerly prods.

"Well, this man was riding an eagle, and he swooped down at me while I was standing on the side of dirt road and said to me that I must find my son, it is time."

"Wow!" Darren exclaims.

Lucy continues, "This man on the eagle, after bareling down at me, kept riding off to the west, and he passed the border sign to Arizona, and he yelled back to me, 'Find my people and you will be healed!'"

The van goes silent and chills run down the backs of Darren, Rachel, and Lucy. They know that they must go to Arizona and find Robert's people and Lucy's son. Darren sits back in his chair in awe, wondering how this has all come about. Why me? he asks himself. Why me at this time with my young family?

Rachel looks in the rearview mirror, noticing Darren's pondering face, and asks, "Darren, are you okay?"

"Sweetheart, yes, I am okay," Darren replies and then thinks about Lucy and Daryl and is concerned with how she might be feeling. He asks her, "Lucy, how are you doing?"

"I am sad to think we don't know where Daryl is," she responds, "and I am praying constantly that he is okay and not harmed. I don't know what I would do without him. Also, I am saddened every time I think about Eric, my sweet boy. Oh, how sweet he was, and I just don't know what happened. Every time I replay the scenario in my mind when he left and we did not hear from him anymore, well, not directly, breaks my heart."

"I'm so sorry," Rachel empathizes.

"Thanks, Rachel,"

"I'm sorry, too," Darren states. "I am sure that we will find Eric soon and Daryl will be okay."

"Thanks, Darren," Lucy says. "I sure hope so."

OWN from the cave opening on the hillside, Eric and Cassie sit on top of a flat rock behind a large tree scanning the abandoned farmhouse below, looking for signs of anybody nearby but not seeing anyone. Cassie, holding Eric's hand tightly, feels nervous. Eric, surveying the parameters like a lion in the faraway tall grass waiting for the right moment to swiftly move in for the kill, and with everything seeming quiet, quickly whispers, "Let's go." He stands up with newfound energy and helps raise Cassie from the rock. "Let's stay in the trees as long as we can until we get closer to the house," he softly says. They move cautiously and listen for any peculiar noises. Arriving fifty feet away from the old homestead, they hide behind a piney tree surrounded by tall brush. Eric peeks his head around the tree, being able to see the front of the house. The green minivan that they arrived in is still parked in front with another red car parked beside it. He moves his head out a little further, and a slender woman with long red hair suddenly walks out the front entrance. Eric moves his head back behind the tree.

They hear a door open and close and a car start, pulling out and driving away. After a few moments, Eric carefully pokes his head out from behind the tree again, and the red car is missing but the minivan is still there. He turns and whispers to Cassie, "Let's go for it." Still holding each other's hands, they briskly move out from behind the tree and begin to walk forward. Arriving at the side of the house, Eric pauses, glances around, and listens— hearing nothing. "Okay, let's move to the car and see if the keys are in it," Eric says. They bend, hunched over, rushing to the van, hoping to be less visible. Reaching the van, Eric carefully opens the driver-side door, trying to not make any noise. The keys are in the ignition. He gently gets in sitting down on the cushioned seat, leaving the door open in case of a quick getaway, while Cassie bends down, hiding herself, behind the open door. Eric turns the key, and the vehicle starts. "Hurry, get in the car," he whispers down to Cassie. As Cassie quickly opens the passenger-side door, a tall woman with short, black hair comes running out of the house, yelling, "Hey!"

"Jump in!" Eric shouts.

Cassie jumps into the vehicle headfirst while Eric puts the van in reverse, peeling out backwards. He slams onto the brakes and turns the steering wheel, spinning the van around forward. Cassie's feet are dangling from the vehicle. He puts the minivan into drive and pushes on the accelerator as she is able to scoot her way into the vehicle. In a fury, they drive off.

Taking no chances that anyone could be following them, Eric drives fast through the winding road. Eventually coming to a T in the road, he turns left. The road comes to another T and he goes right. He drives for another mile, not seeing another house, building, or car around. As they come to the end of the road, he can see that it swerves to the right, and it looks like there might be a main road just beyond the bend. As they drive to the bend and turn slightly right, another car passes them, watching Eric and Cassie drive speedily by. The car screeches to a stop, goes into reverse, and turns around, following Eric and Cassie.

"Uh oh," Eric says.

Cassie looks back and says, "Yup, they are following us. Hurry!"

Eric steps on the gas. They arrive at an intersection, and as the light turns yellow and then red, Eric yells, "Hold on!" Cassie pushes her head back onto the seat and braces herself for the worst as they barrel through it safely. The car behind does not stop, racing through the intersection at top speed, not willing to give up the chase. As the car passes the light and enters the middle of the intersection, a big dump truck drives through the intersection, slamming into the side of the car and crushing it flat like a foot slamming onto the top of a pop can.

Eric and Cassie speed away, leaving the reservation going towards Phoenix. When they arrive in Phoenix they find a motel to stay the night and park the minivan a few blocks away at an abandoned building, walking to the motel, hoping that if someone is to spot the vehicle, they will not know where they are.

Inside the motel and after taking a shower, Cassie gets dressed, walks out of the bathroom, and sits down on the edge of the bed next to Eric, who is watching the nightly news. She gives him a soft kiss on the cheek and then jokingly asks, "Anything on the news about us?"

He smiles and says, "I don't see anything, but that does not mean much."

"For sure," she states and then asks, "Do you think you could find that place on the reservation again if you had to?"

"Of course," Eric confidently responds.

"How do you know that place?" she asks, inquisitively.

"Before I met you, I spent some time on the reservation searching for answers to my family."

"I know you don't like talking much about your family," she says with understanding.

"I didn't," he states in matter of fact, "but I guess things have changed now."

Cassie sits, silently waiting for Eric to explain, but he then says, "Something happened down there in that cave that altered something inside me."

"What happened?" she asks.

Eric turns the volume down on the television and places the remote on the bed, stating, "I was taken some place."

"What place?"

"Somewhere with tall cedars and a luscious garden in the middle of them. It was such a serene place, but, yet there was confusion in the air—I could feel it."

"Confusion?"

"Yes," he states, "I think the confusion was my inner turmoil; it was as though this place would reflect my thoughts and feelings, what I was truly feeling—the condition of my heart. However, the place did not change, meaning the serenity of the place."

"Huh," Cassie says, puzzled.

"Yes, interesting," Eric says and then stares straight ahead, "And then it happened."

"What?"

He pauses, remembering to himself the wonder of the moment, then continues, "He came to me. He came from behind and within the trees. It was a man with a white beard wearing a white, worn cloth. He came to me with piercing blue eyes and said that he was watching me and that he knew that I was hurt." Eric clears his throat. "I said to him that I wasn't hurt. I felt fine. He then took his right hand and touched my forehead, healing any sickness within me. A love then permeated the air, coming right through me, that was undeniable, and an enduring peace that one cannot truly describe entered me." Eric's eyes begin to swell with tears, feeling overpowered by emotion.

"Wow," Cassie remarks. She leans over and gives him a hug, commenting, "What a wonderful experience!"

"Yes, words can't really explain the feeling," Eric says with reverence. He then gives her a romantic kiss.

E don't have much gas!" Rachel exclaims, in a panic while driving eighty miles per hour on the highway.

"How much?" Darren asks, wanting to know exactly.

"Almost on empty."

"Okay, let's stop at the next exit with gas," he directs.

"Daddy," Stephanie says with scare in her voice, "are we going to be okay?"

"Yes, of course," Darren assures her.

Roger then expresses, "I don't want to die."

"Oh, my boy," Darren says with emphasis, "don't say things like this. We will all be fine."

John asks, "Dad, what are we going to do?"

"Not sure, son, but I have an idea," Darren pauses and says louder, "I think they are after me. Robert, from the bus, gave me something and I think they, whoever they are, are after it."

"Do you think it is the same people who have Daryl?" Lucy anxiously asks.

"Not sure, but it makes sense. So, my idea is that when we get to the gas station I'll drop you off, and you guys run in and hurry and call 911, and I'll keep driving."

"No way!" Rachel cries in fierce disagreement. "We are not leaving one another!"

"I think they will follow me."

"We are not separating again!"

"Listen," Darren states calmly, "This might be our only chance to get help."

"Why not give what Robert gave you to these people?" Rachel inquires with haste.

"I really don't think," Darren comments, "that these guys want to be caught. And we are not giving away what Robert gave me. He asked me to keep it safe, and that we will do. So if we buy some time to get help, it might work."

Rachel, knowing her husband, that when he is serious about something, there is not much she or anyone can do to bend his will. With utter disagreement, she sighs, "Ahhh," moving on. She glances down at the gas meter and the red *E*, signifying "empty," now shines. She cries, "We better get somewhere quick; we are on empty!"

"We now have about twenty to thirty minutes," Darren states.

Lucy shouts, "Look! An exit ten miles away!"

"So," Darren says, "any other ideas?"

The van stays quiet. After a few moments, Lucy softly replies, "Okay," knowing that even though the idea sounds logical, it's still extremely risky. Rachel hesitates to say anything because she knows that there is not much more to be said; her husband has made up his mind, and there is nothing that she or anyone can say to change it. Darren feels Rachel's hesitancy and expresses to her with reassurance, "Rachel, sweetheart, it keeps all of you safer and gives us a chance to possibly get help. I think it will work."

Lucy offers her opinion: "Rachel, it does not seem like they want to hurt us, or they would have done it already. They want people alive."

Rachel, stewing amongst her emotions, quietly responds, "Okay, but I'm not happy with this."

"Sweetheart," Darren states, "I know it is not ideal, but it is better to give you all a chance at being safe than anything else. They want what I have."

They drive the next few miles in silence, continually looking backwards, checking on the car behind them. As they get a thousand feet from the exit, Darren says, "Okay, so Rach, when we pull off the freeway, I will change spots with you."

"Okay," Rachel says, still feeling upset.

Lucy positively comments, "Okay, here goes nothing."

Reaching the exit, Rachel veers off the freeway, slowing down. Darren stands up, reaches over the center console and grabs onto the steering wheel with his right hand. Rachel lays her seat back and slides up and out, falling over into the back of the van. Darren slides into the driver's seat. He pushes on the gas pedal to pick up speed and looks out the rearview mirror. The car is a hundred feet behind them. Arriving at the stop sign at the top of the exit, he looks both ways and gradually rides through it, turning right. "Great, let's get ready," he says. "Okay, I'll stop right in front of the entrance and you guys run in and call 911, and get help right away! I will keep driving off and see if I can't get them to follow me!"

With the kids behind her, Rachel places her hand on the van door's handle ready to move fast while Lucy holds onto the front door handle, ready to open it. Darren rolls up to the gas station's entrance and stops. Lucy, Rachel, and the kids race out of the van and run inside. Darren pulls away. The car that is following them drives by the station and follows Darren.

"It worked!" Darren shouts to himself. "It really worked!"

Knowing that he has only maybe fifteen or twenty minutes remaining before running out of gas, and the next service station is probably forty to fifty minutes ahead, he starts thinking of what to do next. He thinks, When I run out of gas do I run for it? No. Do I go until I run out of gas and then wait in the car until they come and get me? Maybe.

With the combination between furiously thinking in an unusually stressful situation and the adrenaline now being pumped into his veins, Darren's right foot is unconsciously pushing down on the gas pedal—accelerating his speed—eighty-five, eighty-six, eighty-seven, eighty-eight, eighty-nine, ninety, ninety-one, ninety-two, ninety-three miles per hour. Darren glances in the rearview mirror back at the car, and it is right up to the bumper. "What the heck!" Darren shouts. "What are these guys trying to do?" The van then violently shocks forward being bumped from behind. "What the heck!" he yells again. "Are they trying to kill me?" He steps on the accelerator, trying to distance himself from them. *Bang!*

Bang! Two gunshots are heard, and the back tires are shot; the van immediately starts to swerve out of control, heading for the center median. In an effort to keep the vehicle on the road, Darren jerks the steering wheel back to the right, overcorrecting. The van flies up into the air, flipping, spinning, and violently tumbling into the dirt-filled center. Darren's body is thrown from the driver's seat window, slamming hard onto the ground, instantly going unconscious.

The men in the car slowly drive up to the mangled and crumbled mess. Seeing Darren's bloody body lying motionless in the median twenty yards behind the destroyed vehicle, they stop. Two men from the back seat get out and walk over to Darren. As they reach him, one man bends down and feels Darren's pulse—he is still breathing. The man stands up and yells back to the car, "He's still alive!" The driver shouts in response, "Hurry! Pick him up and put him in the trunk!" The two men lift Darren up off the ground and carry him back to the car. They slide him into the trunk and slam the door shut. They drive off with nobody witnessing the wreckage.

A T 7:00 a.m., the motel wake-up call rings, startling Eric awake. He reaches out with his left hand and picks up the phone's handset, dropping it back down onto the switch hook, quieting the call. Without thinking, he automatically reaches with his right hand across the bed, feeling for Cassie, but his fingers only touch empty cloth sheets, thus provoking a quickened tinge of anxiety. Eric sluggishly opens his eyes, moving them from the bed to the covered window, then, down to the chair in the corner of the room, seeing Cassie's slender legs crossed while the one on top is steadily bouncing like a metronome counting the beats to music, creating a sense of relief within him, knowing she is safe. Cassie is dressed and ready for the day.

"Wow," Eric mumbles still half asleep. "Glad to see you."

"How are you feeling?" she asks.

"I'm exhausted."

"I bet you are."

"Give me a few more minutes and I'll get up, okay?"

"Take your time."

Watching Eric wake up, Cassie starts to think about the time when they first met. Both worked in Seattle at a corporate financial institution: she in customer service and he in accounting. Their company had a social night one weekend at a nearby pub where they both attended. Throughout the night and from the corner of her eye, Cassie kept noticing Eric glance at her from across the bar. As the night drew on, Eric finally walked over to Cassie and said with straight forwardness, "Hello, my name is Eric, and I'd love to take you out one night."

Cassie smiled, and with unexpected wit responded, "We are out tonight. Where do you want to go?"

"Anywhere," Eric replied.

They left the gathering and found themselves in a twenty-four-hour diner talking and laughing the whole night while eating pancakes and slurping down ice cream shakes. Through the conversation, it dawned on them that they both had the same birthdays, but Eric was two years older. From that day on, they dated and shortly fell in love.

Sometime after Eric began feeling disenfranchised by corporate America and a bit unsettled and bored with life. He decided to leave work and go "traveling"—be homeless for a time. Telling Cassie about his decision, she, without parents or siblings at the time, decided to follow him. She was an only child, and both of her parents had passed away; her father from pancreatic cancer and her mother from a sudden stroke. Eric had become her family. They packed up their belongings in backpacks and took to the streets.

They roamed rural Washington for two years, moving from different odd job to odd job, farm to farm, working for cash or a place to stay—abandoned houses, rundown shacks, or an empty bedroom in someone's house. As carefree living as it seemed for them, the time homeless did not come without its serious drawbacks—Eric became hooked on drugs. After the rain of the Northwest had drenched their souls in what seemed like a cloudy coldness, they decided it was the right time to start over and get away from the weather and the negative-influence friends that had been accumulated. They sought a warmer climate, so moving south to the arid desert of Phoenix, Arizona, they went.

Arizona soon became home to them. They both got jobs in local restaurants, Cassie as a server and Eric a cook. They rented a small studio and, as normal as things were becoming, Eric however, still battled the snatching war with drugs.

Sitting in the burgundy motel chair, Cassie watches Eric rise from bed. She thinks he is so cute, always has thought that, even if it is with bed hair and his voice sounding groggy as a frog. Eric walks to the bathroom and takes a long-overdue hot shower to clean and freshen up for the day. Watching the steam ooze from underneath the bathroom door and listening to Eric sing the Beatles song "All You Need Is Love," Cassie can't help but feel a joyful gratitude for his miraculous, healthy recovery.

Eric, fully dressed, exits the bathroom and sits on the end of the bed. He asks Cassie, "Okay, what do you think we do from here?"

Cassie, smiling, stands up from the chair and walks over to the bed, sitting down next to him. They give each other a loving and tender kiss. Eric gently places his hand on her right knee, and she slides her hand over his shoulders to be closer to him, saying, "I am not sure. What are you thinking? It seems like the blind is leading the blind, huh?"

Eric replies, "Of course not, Sherlock!"

She giggles, saying, "Well, okay, if I'm Sherlock, I have an idea."

"Okay, Watson awaits."

"We know that we need to find your dad and mom, and that they were living in Denver last, but we aren't sure if they are still there or not. It has been a while. So we should first try to reach out to them and go from there. We also know that there are people following us, so we need to be careful."

"Sherlock, you're brilliant."

"I know," she comments with a grin.

"Okay," he states, "This is what I'm thinking."

"Sounds like Watson is back to his normal thinking self."

"No, only here to assist the real Sherlock."

"Of course, but please, Watson," Cassie remarks, "I insist."

"It would be nice to call my parents," Eric states, "but I can't remember their phone number."

"Do you remember any phone numbers from home or anybody that might know their phone number?"

Eric stares at the white wall in front, pondering, and then responds, "It has been so long since I have talked with anybody from home but, actually, I do remember my sister's phone number because we talked two years ago, but don't know if it is still the same."

"Sounds good, Watson."

"You are beautiful, Sherlock!"

"You're not so bad looking yourself, Watson."

Eric stands up and walks over to the phone, dialing the front desk.

"Hello," a lady says.

"Hello," Eric says happily, "are we allowed to make long-distance calls on this phone?"

"Local calls only," she replies. "You have to pay in advance for long-distance calls."

"Okay, thanks," Eric hangs up the phone. He turns to Cassie and says, "Hun, we have a couple hundred bucks left in cash, right?"

"Yes."

"I'll go down and put some credit on this phone to make a call, being that you don't have your cell phone anymore."

"Yeah, it fell out of my back pocket when we were being chased from that abandoned house. Please be careful. We know people will be looking for us."

"I know," Eric says and walks down to the front desk. He pays the lady at the front desk and starts walking back up to the room, noticing a black SUV slowly driving by. Eric quickly jolts behind a car that is parked in a parking stall and hunches behind it. Once the SUV passes by, he rushes to the room and opens the door, breezing inside.

"Is everything okay?" Cassie asks with concern.

"I think it is them."

"Who?"

"Those people who were following us, or, at least, those people who had us before—those people." He continues, "a car was driving by, a black SUV. I hid behind a parked car outside and hurried inside."

"Okay, we've got to hurry," Cassie expresses hastily.

Eric goes over to the phone and dials the one number that he can remember of his sisters. *Ring, ring, ring, ring,* it goes to voicemail: "Hello, this is Mary. Thanks for calling, and I'll get back to you as soon as I can. Please leave a message." At the beep, Eric leaves a message: "Hello, Mary, it is Eric. I know it has been too long, but I'm calling because I need to talk with you. Can you please call me back as soon as you can on this number?"—he gives her the motel's phone number—"thanks," and hangs up.

Eric stands, staring down at the phone, feeling strange to reach out to family after so much time, but also good to finally do so. "Well," Eric says, "that was a bit difficult, but I sure hope she gets it soon."

"That was great," Cassie states.

"Yeah, it was. It has been too long."

Cassie, sitting in the chair, leans over to the window curtain and peeks out.

"You see anything?" Eric asks.

"No, I don't."

"Hey, Sherlock, what do you think we should do?"

"Watson," Cassie says, "we should wait here for a little bit and see if Mary calls us back, and then go from there."

"Sherlock, you're a true genius!" Eric says, grinning with joy in his heart to have another day with his beautiful wife, even if they are being chased by people they don't know, don't have much money, are using a stolen car, and have no idea where his mom and dad are. He looks at her and is grateful for their relationship, friendship, and her neverending support. They wait for an hour hoping for the phone to ring, but it does not.

"Dear, do you think we should get going?" Eric asks. "I don't know if we should be waiting around too much longer. I think we need to get out of here. They might find that car soon, and then we are going to be sitting pheasants in a field surrounded by hound dogs. We could be in a bigger mess."

"Let's wait for another half-hour."

"Okay."

They wait patiently and sit silently in the dark, not wanting to offer any sign that anyone is in the room. Ten minutes goes by, and Cassie peeks out the curtain again seeing a black SUV parked near the front desk door. "Uh-oh, our hideout might have been blown," she states.

Eric stands up and walks over to the window, opening the curtain a sliver, also seeing the vehicle. He confirms, "Yup, it is time we move."

Eric grabs Cassie's hand and they move to the door. Cautiously opening it, Eric pokes his head outside, scanning in both directions to make sure it is clear to leave the room. It looks safe, so they quickly leave, going around to the back.

Two men with black suits walk out of the motel's front entrance. They get into the SUV and park it a few doors down from where Eric and Cassie were staying. They walk to the room and knock on the door. "Hello," one man says. They wait for a few moments, and when there is no response, the man knocks again. Again, with no response, the man then takes out his gun and shoots the door open. He pushes it open, and the room is empty.

Eric and Cassie jog down the street towards where they parked the van. Coming up to the abandoned building, they slow down, taking deliberate and ready steps in case they need to run away. Their eyes frantically scan the premises for any sudden and unwanted movements. Walking to the corner of the building, they stop and glance around it, seeing the vehicle. With no sign of anyone around, Eric says, "Hurry, let's go and go fast." They dash towards the van, getting in and driving off.

The two men exit the motel room, knowing that Eric and Cassie have escaped. The men hop back into their SUV and drive off, wheels screeching as they exit the parking lot.

J AY stands leaning his thin and slender body up against the stainless-steel fridge in the kitchen of a luxurious apartment in San Francisco, California. His face is long like his body with gray, mysterious eyes. Inside the apartment, the redwood floors are rich in tone, contrasting the white countertops. The cabinets are blue with clear glass displaying expensive fine china plates and tall wine glasses. Burt, who is a large, framed man with speckled eyes, is sitting on a black stool at the kitchen island glaring at Jay.

"It appears that they have lost them," Jay states, "We have the guy from the bus who initially ran away, but we have lost the boy and his wife; don't know where they are for now."

"And?" Burt stoically inquires.

"We think they can't be too far from Phoenix."

"Well?"

"We are moving on it," Jay says. "We haven't found them yet, but we will."

Burt nods his head slightly.

Jay remarks, "Hyrum is dead."

"How?"

"Don't know," Jay replies and then continues, "There were no bullet holes, no markings on his body; appears as though he had some kind of a stroke and chocked on his vomit."

"What happened?"

"Don't really know."

"How do we not know?" Burt demands.

"One minute Hyrum is with the kid and the ladies, and the next minute he is dead—they are now missing."

"All of them?"

"Yes."

"And the driver, the kid?"

"Gone. Disappeared."

With disdain, Burt says, "It's time to call him."

Jay pulls his phone out of his black leather jacket and starts making a phone call.

"Jay-o!" the jovial voice on the other end answers.

"Tip, it is time you get involved."

"Okie-dokie, Jay-o!"

"Meet us in Phoenix."

"Can do-o!" Tip positively expresses.

"When you get your flight, give me a call back."

"Sure thing-o!"

Jay hangs up the phone and places it back into his leather pocket. "Tip is on his way," he states to Burt.

Burt nods his head okay. "Jay, keep an eye on that boy," Burt orders, "You know how he does business. It can get messy."

"Sure thing," Jay responds.

Now, as for the friend and neighbor, Daryl, right?" Burt says, "We sure he doesn't know anything?"

"Duke is saying that he does not know much."

"Then the other one is our guy!" Burt expresses.

"Yes, they are on their way to Phoenix as we speak," Jay says.

"Where are they?" Burt asks.

"In Arizona already."

"Make sure they get there! We need him. He has what we need!"

"Sure thing."

"Time to head to Phoenix," Burt says, "Get us on the next flight there."

S TANDING in the passenger pick up area in the Phoenix airport, a polished, black Ford Explorer rolls up and stops in front of Burt and Jay. Picking up their travel bags, the men walk to the vehicle and place them inside. Both get into the back seat.

"Hey, Jay-o, glad you called-o!" Tip says, sitting in the front passenger seat.

"Yup," Jay responds with no facial expression.

"Where to now-o?" Tip asks.

"Get on the freeway and go north."

"You heard the man, Sam-o, let's go north!"

Sam, the driver, stares forward, driving out of the airport and onto the freeway. After twenty minutes, Jay gives more direction: "Get off on this exit." Sam departs the freeway and Jay commands, "Turn right, then left, and go straight until you reach a hillside gate."

Following Jay's directions, they arrive to a large black metal gate with mounted cameras on top and a speaker box stationed in front. Sam drives up to the box and stops, rolling down the tinted window. He reaches out and pushes the dial button.

A voice asks, "Hello, Burt, is this you?"

"Yup," Sam replies.

"Great, we are expecting you."

The gate opens and they drive up a beautifully gray paved road to an elegant, white, stone house with a spewing humming-bird fountain in the middle of a circlular driveway. At the front entrance, a man in a gray pinstripe suit is waiting their arrival. Sam stops and Tip rolls down his window, saying, "Hey-o, mate!"

The man politely says, "Leave your keys in the car and I'll take it from here."

Tip nods his head and comments, "Sammy, boy, did you hear this mate-o? He-o is going to take it from here-o! Jay-o, we need to do more work together, boys."

The men get out of the vehicle, and the man in the gray pinstripe suit drives it away. As they reach the front door, an elderly lady dressed in proper black-and-white maid clothes greets them cheerfully, "Welcome," and invites them inside.

The entryway floor contains large gray and white marbled squares with a glossy shine. Glass mirrors sheet the walls. The ceiling is a high circular dome painted with a replica of Michelangelo's famous Sistine Chapel scene between God and Adam where both are reaching out to one another. The woman closes the door and walks around the men. She stands and points her hand, inviting them down the light blue arching hallway that is lined with eclectic classical artwork hanging on the walls and says, "This way. He is waiting for you."

The men walk down the hallway as they gaze and marvel at the art. They enter a spacious living room where a shimmering chandelier hangs from the white, crystallized, peeked ceiling; massive windows span the back wall to witness the dry, mountainous landscape canvassing the backdrop outside; three long and fluffy dark blue leather couches stand on soft, white, pillowtop carpet with tan and brown llama rugs meticulously placed in front; the walls are a soft bluish tone and the trim a bright shining white. A kitchen sits directly to the left with dark brown cupboards and a sparkling, earth-tone countertop.

Leisurely sitting on the couch that is facing them is an older gentleman with his legs crossed smoking an expensive cigar and holding a small glass of brandy. His eyes are dark green, displaying a charming countenance—gray wavy hair, thin cheek bones, and a rigid jawline. His face is perfectly proportional. He is wearing a perfectly pressed, white, collared, short-sleeved shirt, expensive blue jeans, and crisp brown leather sandals.

The maid says to the men, "Please be seated."

Burt and Jay walk toward the man as he blows a stringing flare of cigar smoke up into the air, tainting the sparkling crystals above. As they approach him, the man stands up and surprisingly bursts out, "My friends, glad you made it!"

Burt warmly replies, "Tracy, good to see you."

Burt and Jay embrace him like brothers. Tip and Sam stand behind, watching the friendly scene. Tracy sits back down on the couch, and Burt and Jay sit down on one of the other couches. Jay motions to Tip and Sam to sit on the other couch—they do so, cautiously. Tracy has a puzzled expression and asks Burt, "Do I know these guys?"

"No," Burt responds, "this is Tip and Sam, acquaintances of ours."

"Well," Tracy says, "where are you two from?"

Tip responds, "California, mate."

"Oh, pretty boys, huh?"

"Right-o!"

Tracy then turns to Burt and Jay and asks, "How have my boys been doing?

Burt replies, "Okay."

"Good," Tracy says and then gets right down to business, "Where are we at?"

"There has been a bit of a wrinkle," Burt states.

"There always is."

"Robert does not have it."

"Okay."

"We believe he gave it to a guy on the bus with him."

"And?" Tracy asks.

"They are on their way here with him."

"Alright."

"Now," Burt states, "as for the other item."

"Yes."

"We lost it."

Tracy sits up with alert, and the room's atmosphere thickens. His attitude shifts with angst, asking, "What?"

"We lost it," Burt mentions again.

"What? I thought we retrieved it?"

"We did."

"What happened?"

"We are not sure."

"Not sure?" Tracy asks with agitation.

"We are trying to find the people who were with him when he lost it."

"Joey?"

"Gone. Disappeared," Burt clearly states. "He left the van, but don't know what happened to him."

"Hyrum?"

"Dead."

"Dead?" Tracy asks with doubt.

"Yes," says Burt.

"How?"

"Not sure."

"Mystical?" asks Tracy.

"Strange," Burt clarifies.

Tracy takes a smoke and then a drink of his brandy. Letting the liquid hit the bottom of his belly and swirl around, he then asks, "Magic?"

"Don't know."

"Get ready!" Tracy claims as if he knows something they don't.

Burt continues as if ignoring the last comment from Tracy: "We don't know exactly what went on, but we are tracking the young man and a woman that got away from us and were with Hyrum at the time. We believe they are here in Phoenix."

"Okay."

"We have Tip and Sam to help us."

"Well," Tracy states, "Why are they sitting here?"

Burt turns to Jay, saying, "Red, take Tip and Sam, and let's get out there and find Eric and that woman. We need them so that we can find the other guys."

"Got it!" Jay says. He stands up and says to Tip and Sam, "You guys with me!" The three men leave the house. The vehicle is driven back up the driveway, they get in, and, with Sam driving, they leave.

Back in the house, Tracy asks Burt, "Alright, what are you thinking we do?"

"Packet is still here?" Burt inquires.

"Yes."

"Is he still loyal to you?"

"Always."

"Then," Burt states, "Let's call him in and have him get Syrup—it's time."

Tracy immediately calls to the maid, "Mary, can you please send Packet in!"

"Yes, sir," a gentle voice responds from down the hallway.

Within seconds, a short thirty-year-old with long, brown hair enters the room. His hazel eyes are kind, but tiny compared to the rest of his round face. He sits down in the empty couch and says to Tracy, "You called, sir?"

"Packet," Tracy says, "You are a good man."

"Thanks, sir," Packet sincerely responds.

"I want you to take the BMW, and there is a man I want you to go and retrieve." Tracy pauses and continues, "He lives just outside of Phoenix. When you find him, tell him that Tracy sent you."

"No problem," Packet says with exact obedience.

"Here is the address to his place," Tracy recites it to him.

"Okay."

"Put the address in the car's GPS and it will tell you how to get there."

"Got it!"

"Great, thank you, boy." Tracy pauses, takes a drink, and declares, "You are a great human being, filled with a charity that is inspiring. Now, go on up out of here."

Packet stands up and leaves the room.

"Burt," Tracy states, "When Packet reaches him, we will have things in motion. We need those items!"

"How long has it been since you have been with your people?" The elderly man asks Joseph while sitting in another small, fire lit room inside the cave.

"Quite some time," Joseph honestly responds.

"And your family?" the elderly man inquires further.

Joseph glances at his mother and grandma, replying, "A long time." He pauses and then somberly states, "And haven't seen my dad since I left the reservation."

"Why not?" the elderly man frankly questions, not shying away from potential sorrow.

Before Joseph can respond, Linda respectfully states, "He is dead."

Joseph's facial expression turns to sadness. He looks down at the cave's floor, being warmed from the fire in front, and with quiet and faint eyes he begins to feel disappointment that he and his father never reconciled their relationship; even though the memories with his father are filled with pain and hurt. Knowing that he will never see him again in the earthly tabernacle, Joseph searches for any lasting memory of goodness with his father, including laughter, happiness, love, or joy that might offer some warm solace to not only a relatively dark and cold cave but also a relatively dark and cold memory. Hoping for a sun-filled vision to appear in his mind offering something bright to hold on to, he is overcome with a longing drought as nothing comes to his memory.

Linda, who is sitting next to Joseph, notices the dim feelings in her boy. She reaches over and wraps him in her arms, remorsefully, saying, "I'm sorry." Joseph quietly assures his mother, "Mom, it is okay. I knew he probably would not last long with his addictions. What happened to him?"

"We don't really know. I left after you left years ago because the abuse got so bad. I couldn't take the beatings anymore."

"Mom," Joseph says, sympathetically, "I'm sorry."

"No, son," Linda states, "I'm the one who is sorry. I'm sorry for all the hurt and pain that we caused you." She grabs Joseph by the cheeks and, while staring into his eyes and with true sincerity, she pleas, "Can you ever forgive us?"

Joseph answers, "Of course."

"Thank you."

They embrace tenderly.

Misty watches her daughter and grandson holding each other, and with happy tears streaming down her wrinkled face she thinks about the vision, dreams, and whisperings that she has recently received—"It is time to reunite your family"—are coming true.

After the tender embrace and a few moments of silence, the elderly man then moves the conversation along, asking them, "What do you think of your people?"

Misty sharply replies, "Your people or our people?"

"Our people," the man says with a grin, acknowledging Misty's correction.

Misty claims, "Our people are a blessed people. We have lands and so many freedoms. It is incredible, the resources that are at our fingertips. Our people are richly blessed." She pauses and continues, "As such a blessed people, we also have put ourselves in a predicament. Many of us have become lazy and idolatrous, drifting further away from our spiritual gifts. It saddens me that some of our people seek control, power, and money, just like other peoples. Our way of life is beautiful, yet we seem to be pressing harder for the white man's world, starving for private property, possession, and 'more is better.' It appears that many of us want to live in full sway with the hoarders, without pushing back on them that want control and love power and money."

Misty pauses and waits for a response from the elderly man. He offers no words, only an expression that non-verbally communicates calm, intent listening with non-judgment, creating a sense of ease for Misty to continue sharing her honest feelings. She continues, "It is time our people move from dependence toward community independence; remove ourselves completely from handouts that we receive from any outside governmental assistance and be totally freed from the enslaving dependence that handouts create over time. It is hurting our people; we are better than this. It is time we take our independence back and be a people united in spiritual strength for one another. Let's bring the Lord back to our Mother Earth. It is time."

The fire's flames flicker on the elderly man's thin, bronzed skin as he gazes at her. Gradually, his eyes shift downward to the fire with deep thought stamped onto his face. Then, he glances up, looking at Joseph, asking him, "Did you hear what your grandmother said?"

Joseph softly replies, "Yes."

The elderly man then asks Linda, "Did you hear what your mother said?"

"Yes."

The man then recounts a vision: "A long time ago I dreamed a dream. In the dream I came upon three bay horses. They were in the desert starving. I walked up to the horses and asked them, 'Where are we?' The lead mare neighed down at me with deprivation in her black, piercing, soul-filled eyes, 'We are starving!' I viewed the three horses with their rib bones pressed against their gaunt skin, showing extreme hunger, and regretfully expressed, 'Sorry, I don't know how to help you. I don't know where we are.' The lead mare neighed at me again, furiously, 'Yes, you do!' Her response caught me by surprise because, in fact, I did not know where we were. So, I responded truthfully, 'I don't.' She neighed, 'Do you remember when you were a boy hunting for deer in the Switchback Mountains with your grandfather?' Instantaneously, a memory flooded my mind: my grandfather and I were hunting a stout-horned deer that we had tracked since early in the morning. We were hiding downwind, lying amongst tall grasses in an open field waiting for the animal to come around a bend. I kept glancing at my grandfather, whose chin was buried in the plush legumes, ready to follow his lead with any rapid movement or quick instruction. It was now late afternoon, and the sun was in our back pockets. Grandfather put his right finger up to his lips, signaling to be quiet and still. Being gripped into place, he then soundlessly picked up the rifle that was lying between us as a noise came from around the bend. Grandfather pointed the rifle directly ahead through the standing grasses. He aimed and pulled the trigger. We heard something drop in the near distance. Then, with a smile, he wisely stated, 'My boy, the journey is in the stillness of the moments and also in the action of the day.'

"The lead mare then asked me, 'Do you remember this?'

"I nodded yes.

"This is where you are," she firmly said.

"I was in initial shock. The once-rich, green, grass field and life-filled mountains were gone. My heart felt heavy and remorseful. I asked the mare with sorrow, 'How?'

"She replied without answering directly to the question, 'Our people are starving. Will you help us?'

"I winced at her, for I did not understand her meaning.

"She continued, 'Look, my daughter and her son, we are lost, but you can help us—you can help us!'"

The elderly man allows the dream and the moment to take hold of the three in front of him. The eyes of Misty, Linda, and Joseph are stirred with intense meaningful emotion to the dream. The man then continues: "My brother and sisters, I believe you are the three bay horses that I was supposed to find. This dream now makes sense to me. And after hearing the heart of Misty, and her concerns and vision for our people, I know that it is time to unite for further enlightenment and knowledge from the Creator. We have the blanket, but we are missing the medallion. I think Eric and Cassie will find the medallion, and we will be ready to unite our people together."

"Okay," Misty says through joyful tears. She, too, thinks it is time.

TIP, who is sitting in the front passenger seat of the vehicle next to Sam, who is driving, asks Jay, who is sitting in the back seat, "What you thinkin' man? Where to now?"

Jay's phone suddenly rings, and he answers, "Charlie, what do you got?"

"We found the minivan. Nobody is in it," Charlie declares.

"Where?"

"Next to the downtown bus station."

"Be there in a bit. Stay put!"

Jay says to Tip and Sam, "They found the vehicle at the bus station with nobody in it."

Tip questions, doubtfully, "Mate, really, why would they take the bus out of Phoenix?"

Ignoring Tip's question and its implications, Jay directs, "Let's get there and check it out."

After a short while they drive up to the bus station and see Charlie and his crew, two other guys, parked in a black SUV up the street from Eric and Cassie's empty van as they are staking it out. Charlie points forward to the green minivan that is in a parking stall down on the side of the street. Jay motions for him and his crew to stay in the vehicle.

Sam drives around the station and parks. "Sam, stay here," Jay orders as he and Tip step out. They begin walking to the entrance, and Jay's phone begins to ring. Jay answers and Charlie emphatically says, "They just got back in the van!"

Jay stops, and Tip stops next to him. Jay thinks that this does not make much sense; Eric and his wife know that we are looking for their vehicle; why would they come downtown, park, and get back into the van? He quickly asks Charlie, "What do they look like?"

"It looks like them."

"How tall is the man?

"Oh, it looks like his height."

"How tall?" Jay demands.

"Six feet, two inches."

"And the woman?"

"Five feet, six inches."

Fitting Eric's and Cassie's heights, Jays says, "Wait a second! Let's see what they do!"

Waiting thirty seconds, Jay asks, "Have they left?"

"No, they are just sitting."

"Have the others check it out!"

The two other guys in Charlie's car get out of the vehicle and walk down the street toward the minivan. When they are directly across the street from the van, they turn and take three steps into the street. The man and woman quickly get out of the van and start running for the station's entrance. The men run after them.

Charlie yells over the phone, "They are on the move, running toward the front!"

Jay and Tip start running, turn the corner, and reach the front entrance before the man and woman enter, stopping them. The two men run up behind them, and the man and woman are sandwiched between the four men. The man quickly takes off his ball cap, showing his face and hair.

Jay states while breathing heavy, "I knew it wasn't you. I knew it."

The man and woman stand out of breath, panting for air.

"How much did they pay you?" Jay asks them.

"Oh, not much," the man replies, "but it is more than we can make on the corner of the street, so we took it."

Jay commands, "Hand over the money or we will take you with us."

"Don't have it," the man states clearly.

"What do you mean that you don't have it?"

"We stashed it somewhere else. They told us that you guys might ask for it, so we don't have it on us. And don't try killing us either, because neither me or my babe don't got family or much around, and so not much you can do to us."

Exactly at this moment a bus takes off from the station and Jay glances over at it with a hunch that Eric and Cassie might be in it. He thinks, Oh, you guys think you are pretty smart—if we can find Robert, we will have no problem finding the both of you. Jay gives orders to the others, "Let's walk around the premises—check every nook and cranny, got it?"

Jay calls Charlie while walking away. He answers, and Jay says, "Stay tight. We've been played."

Jay hangs up, and his phone then rings—it is Burt calling from Tracy's place.

"Yeah," Jay answers.

"Jay," Burt states, "Bring in the boys."

"What?" Jay responds, surprised.

"Jay, you heard me. Bring the boys in."

"Okay."

Jay stops and looks all around, thinking of Eric and Cassie. "We will find you," he says to himself. He then remarks to Tip, "We're going back in."

"Going back in?"

"You heard me."

Tip shakes his head and raises his eyebrows in suspicion.

P ACKET parks the BMW at the desired destination, and walks up to the bungalow's rustic wooden front door as vines cover the outside front wall. As he is about to knock, the doorknob turns. A man who resembles Santa Claus with a long white beard, round face, red cheeks, and bluish gray eyes pokes around the door.

"Who are you?" the man inquires.

Packet, feeling nervous, takes a gulp of saliva, and answers, "Tracy told me to come for you."

The man opens the door wider and walks away, inviting Packet inside, "Come in!"

Packet enters through the shorter doorway and shuts the door behind him. The tiny abode sings clean simplicity: white, plastered, palleted walls lean slightly inward with two black-and-white pictures of a team of draft horses and a young man plowing a field hang unlevel on opposite sides of the room at chest height; a scraggly, red rug covers the middle of the wooden-floored room with a brown reclining chair in the corner; a brass lamp is turned on, standing in between the chair and a wide, black bookcase filled with an extensive selection of books. Standing inside, Packet smells something delicious coming from a doorway without a door and hinges leading to the kitchen—perfuming the place with hominess. The stout man walks from the kitchen through the small door frame, barely fitting, with a white rag draped over his palm, displaying two fresh pieces of homemade bread topped with hand-harvested butter and honey.

"Sit down, please, sit down," the man demands jovially.

Walking over to the reclining chair, Packet sits down and sinks down into its soft cushion.

"Here, here," the man cheerfully states, "Try this and tell me what you think—you'll never have anything better." He offers a piece of bread on the rag to Packet in such a graceful and inviting manner that it makes him feel a bit uncomfortable: he does not initially trust such kindness from strangers. Packet timidly reaches out and takes the piece of bread. The man then walks to the kitchen and brings in a maplewood chair, plopping it in the middle of the room, sitting down. Packet hesitates to take a bite, graciously waiting for the man to eat first. The man demands, "So, go ahead, don't be shy, boy!"

Before taking a bite, Packet deliberately inhales the fresh and natural smells that encompass the quaint surroundings, creating a home-like sensation within him that he hasn't felt in a long time. Wow, he thinks, There is something here that is incredibly refreshing.

The man sits, staring at him with a childlike grin, anxiously anticipating his first-taste expression, the honest tastebud reaction—measuring instant satisfaction for all culinary activists. This expression, he hopes, shows the igniting of the tongue and mouth with a delicate balance between explosive yet caressed gratification, telling a story mixed with care, preparation, and creativity, ultimately ending in riotous cheering for the apex of existence upon reaching the stomach. Packet's eyes open brightly after taking a bite. He swallows and exhales with deep amusement as his facial muscles pull upward to a large, glowing grin. Packet's every bite thereafter is taken with gratitude. The man is reassured once again that he, indeed, can bake a delicious batch of homemade bread.

After Packet finishes eating, the man states, "Here, I'll take the rag."

Packet hands him the rag and says, "Thank you very much. It was delicious."

The man smiles, takes the rag, and walks back into the kitchen, dumping it into the sink. He returns and plops himself back into the chair, asking, "So, what does Tracy want?"

"Don't know. He told me to come get you."

"Come get me?"

"Yeah, that is what he told me to tell you."

"Well, do you know why you are here, kid?"

"No," Packet responds succinctly.

"He found the items, didn't he?"

Packet is bewildered by the question because he does not know what the man is talking about.

Seeing the expression on Packet's face, the man says, "You have no idea what I'm talking about, do you, youngster?"

"No."

The man walks to the bookcase and retrieves a book with an antiquated, worn-out, leather covering. He sits back down in the chair and places the book on his thigh, holding it tenderly from its edges. The man kindly asks, "My boy, what is your name?"

"Robert, but they call me Packet."

"Hum?" the man sighs with intrigue. "Packet, huh?"

"Yup."

"Well, okay, Robert, my boy," the man says, "Do you know what this book is on my lap?"

"No."

"Have you ever seen anything like it?"

"Not sure."

"Not sure?" the man asks, inquisitively.

"Yeah," Packet states, "When I was young, I saw a book like this in my parent's house underneath their bed."

"Really?" The man asks, feeling deeply intrigued to understand.

"Yeah, I was young," Packet says, "and my siblings and me were playing hide-and-go-seek in the house. I went and hid underneath my parent's bed, and there was a white cloth covering something. I lifted the cloth just a little and saw a book similar to that one. I quickly put the cloth back over it because I did not want to get in trouble."

"Huh," the man comments quietly. "Did you ever see the book again?"

"No, I never did."

"Okay," the man says, "How old were you when you saw this book?"

"Can't really remember, but oh, maybe four years old."

"And what is your and Tracy's connection?"

"Let's just say that Tracy saved my life."

"Wow!" the man gasps. "How?"

"I was fifteen years old and had run away from home. I was living on the streets for a while and was mixing with a pretty rough crowd when Tracy showed up and brought me in; he fixed me a up a bit."

"And you say that your name is Robert?"

"Yes."

"And your last name?"

"Albright, Tracy's last name."

"And your given last name?"

Packet hesitates because he hasn't said his biological last name in years. He then timidly says, "Hanson."

The man pauses, staring at the young man with a blank expression as unexpected emotions immediately swirl upward from his gut. His eyes faintly blink as certain picture-memories enter his mind like watching a movie reel pass by in seconds. He leans back into his chair, now inherently holding onto the book with a tighter grip. He inhales and exhales deeply, trying to wash away the particles of a painful history from his face.

Packet sits, watching the man's reaction, realizing that the mention of his last name made a profound effect and is stacked with layers of meaning—he wonders why. He sits, hoping he will soon understand the sudden, non-verbal facts of this moment.

The air in the room thickens. The man gathers his senses and straightens back up in the chair. He says intently, "Albright," acting as if nothing happened, and then stands up, taking the book back to the shelf.

"Wait," Packet expresses, "What about the book?"

"Oh, never mind," says the man, "I think it is time we go see Tracy." He gently places the book on the shelf and walks back into the kitchen, shouting, "I'll be ready in five minutes!"

Five minutes go by, and the man walks through the doorway with a black duffle bag in hand and a new attire: tan khakis, sandals, and a white t-shirt with a saying in dark red, "If you mean it, then you better say it!" He says, "Let's go!"

Packet stands up from the recliner, and they both walk to the front door. The man opens the door for Packet to leave, and before he exits, he asks, "So, what is your name, anyways?"

"They call me Syrup."

"Why?"

"Because you tasted how sweet my stuff is."

Packet grins, and they leave. While in the car Syrup's mood shifts, appearing solemn, quiet, almost ashamed. Arriving at Tracy's, they walk into the main living room and sit down on the blue couches waiting for Tracy to enter. Tracy walks in and notices that Syrup seems depressed.

"Hey, Syrup!" Tracy exclaims, "Gosh, it has been some time!"

Avoiding eye contact and now with a sunken frame, Syrup quietly says, "You, too."

Tracy sits on the couch that is perpendicular to them and states, "So, we have one item."

"Really?" Syrup says with more excitement as his body language perks up.

"Yup," Tracy says, "Well, we think we have the one, but as for the other, we think we will have it in no time."

"I told you to come and get me when you have both!" Syrup remarks loudly, with agitation.

"Yeah, I know," Tracy confirms, "But we couldn't wait for this. We have to move now, and fast."

"Why?" Syrup asks with further frustration to his tone.

"Because we think we have the one, and as for the other, we will have it soon, and when we do, I want us to be ready."

Syrup shakes his head in disfavor. Tracy ignores him and says, "So, I'm thinking you can stay here in the guest room until we have everything in order and prepare what we need. I don't want to be wasting any time."

Syrup again shakes his head back and forth, now more slowly and in dramatic fashion, commenting, "You have always been this way—too overzealous!"

Again, ignoring Syrup's reactions, Tracy asks, "How long for you to prepare everything?"

"Oh, maybe a couple of days if I have everything that I need," Syrup states, despondently.

"What is it that you need?"

Syrup hesitates and asks, "Won't this be better discussed in private?"

"Private?" Tracy asks with impatience. "Heck, this is private!"

"Are you sure?" Syrups asks, doubting.

"Yes," Tracy claims with certainty.

Syrup glances at Packet and then back at Tracy, and asks again with an underlying tone of uncertainty, "Are you sure we know who we are dealing with?"

"Of course," Tracy states clearly, "Come on now, Syrup, what is the problem? What are you worried about, and why such melancholy?"

Not wanting to answer the question directly, Syrup comments, "I think we better have this conversation in private, Tracy."

"No!" Tracy cries. "We are fine! Heck, Syrup, we have been waiting for this moment for a long time, and what is the problem?"

"Tracy," Syrup states, "I'm telling you that I won't discuss this anymore until we have some privacy."

"Oh! Syrup, you always were a little bit on the unbelieving side, way too cautious, come on, get with the program—we are fine."

Syrup pauses and glances again back at Packet. He then looks at Tracy and respectfully says, "Tracy, we need to talk in private."

"Oh, my gosh!" Tracy yells and then orders, "Packet, can you please leave the room, so I can console my old doubting Thomas here!"

Packet respectfully stands from the couch and starts walking out of the room. As he is about to turn the corner to go down the hallway, he turns, looking back at Syrup, who is looking right at him with eyes that warrant serious caution.

ACHEL and Lucy are sitting across from Sheriff Terry Burdow's desk in the Durango, Colorado, police station. Sheriff Burdow is a bald, short, plump man with a large belly. His black eyes are hard to read—stiff. "Let me see if I have this right," he says to the ladies. "You were being followed by some guys and you get out of your car and those guys, you think, are now following your husband?"

"Yes," Rachel eagerly responds, knowing that they are pressed against time.

Sheriff Burdow questions Lucy, "Ma'am, this is your story, too, but they have your husband?"

"Yes."

"So, both of your husbands are missing and possibly have been taken by these people who were following you?"

"We told you all this last night," Rachel asserts with consternation. "Why are you stalling us?"

"Ladies," Sheriff Burdow respectfully says, "Your stories match and the kids' stories all match."

"I know," Rachel exclaims, now with great annoyance for this redundancy.

"Huh," the sheriff comments while rubbing his chubby chin. "Any more information?"

Rachel and Lucy say emphatically in unison, "No!"

"Well," Sheriff Budrow states to Rachel, "We found and identified the van that supposedly your husband was driving."

"And?" Rachel says with anticipation, "Did you find my husband, Darren?"

"No, we did not," the sheriff pauses and then continues, "the vehicle was totaled."

"Oh no!" Rachel gasps in horror.

"Ma'am, in fact, your husband is nowhere to be found."

Rachel remains silent while Lucy reaches over and holds her hand for comfort from the sudden bad news.

"The back tires were shot," the sheriff then states. "It appears the vehicle spun out of control and your husband was thrown from the vehicle. However, where we think he would have probably landed there is no body."

"No body!" Rachel shrieks and drops her head in terror. Lucy puts her arm around her as she begins to cry.

The sheriff grabs some tissues from the desk drawer and hands them to Rachel. He asks, "Ladies, is there anyone else who might have more information?"

Lucy replies soberly, "Mary, my daughter, let's call her again."

"We talked to her last night, and she had not heard anything," the sheriff states.

"I know," Lucy says, "but maybe she has heard something since then."

"Okay, and where is she right now?"

"Still in Denver," Lucy replies.

"Okay, let's call her." The sheriff pulls the receiver off the phone on the desk and dials her number. The phone rings a few times and Mary answers, "Hello."

"Mary," the sheriff says, "This is Sheriff Burdow again from Durango. I'm sitting here with your mother and Rachel." He pauses and continues, "They are okay. We are reaching out again to see if anyone has reached out to you since last night."

"Yes, my brother called this morning."

The sheriff asks with vigor, "When?"

"This morning," she repeats, annoyed.

"Okay, what did he say?" the sheriff asks, enthusiastically.

Mary hesitates, not trusting Sheriff Burdow's tone, asking, "Why?"

"Mary, you know why. Your father and Darren are missing. We found the van that Darren was driving, and he has disappeared.

We need more information. If your brother knows something or can help lead us to those who maybe have them—we need that information."

"Let me talk to my mom," Mary orders, still not believing the sheriff.

"Mary, your mother is right here."

"Great, give her the phone."

"Mary," Sheriff Budrow states, asking again, "What did he say?"

"Put my mom on the phone right now!" she orders, angrily.

The sheriff acquiesces and hands Lucy the phone. Lucy leans over in her chair and takes the phone, asking, "Hello, Mary?"

"Yes, Mom," Mary says, "Are you, Rachel, and the kids okay?"

"Yes," Lucy responds kindly. "Everything is okay, still staying at the local hotel, and everything is okay. They brought us in again."

After Mary is assured, she abruptly says, "Eric called me this morning."

Lucy's eyes grow big like the sun and her facial expression shines with hope as her voice raises with relief, saying like a parent who has longed to see her son, "Wow!"

"I know, Mom," Mary states, "It has been some time."

"Way too long," Lucy emphasizes as she begins to cry.

The sheriff reaches over the desk and hands her tissues as well, shaking his head in disbelief, watching the exchange. "What did he say?" Lucy asks.

"He left a message saying that he needed to talk. He called from a number that is not ringing anymore."

"Huh," Lucy remarks, sensing that it is strange.

"I know, Mom. Weird things are happening."

"Yes," Lucy confirms, wondering why her son would call.

"Should I go to Sheriff Redlock's station here at home and talk with him about Eric, you, Dad, Rachel, and Darren?" Mary asks.

"Yes, please do," Lucy responds. "He tried helping us when Eric went missing. We trust him."

"Okay, will do, Mom."

Lucy tenderly states, "Love you, Mary, please be safe."

"Okay, Mom, you guys, too. Hopefully we find Dad and Darren soon, and if Eric reaches out again, I'll let you know."

"Okay, sweetheart, sounds great."

"Mom, let me talk to the sheriff again."

"Okay, sweetheart, love you."

"Love you, too, Mom."

Lucy hands the phone to Sheriff Burdow, and he puts the receiver up to his ear. Mary clearly states, "I will get hold of Sheriff Redlock from our area and have him call you."

"Who?"

"Sheriff Larry Redlock from the Arapahoe County police department."

"Why not tell me what Eric said?"

"We will work through Sheriff Redlock from now on!" Mary asserts with an unbridled command.

"But Mary," the sheriff says desperately—the phone hangs up.

SHERIFF Larry Redlock in the Arapahoe County, Colorado, police station sits behind his black walnut desk in his office. He's tall, wiry, and wears black-rimmed glasses contrasting his serious hazel eyes. His rigid jawline reaches his square chin from an almost perfect right angle. Mary sits across from his desk.

"How long ago did you say your brother called you, Mary?" the sheriff asks.

"It was this morning," Mary answers, "Yeah, out of the blue. I tried calling the number back a couple of times, and nobody answered. I then tried later a few more times and still no answer!"

"What number did you say it was?"

Mary tells the sheriff the phone number. He writes it down on an eight by eleven-inch yellow notepad, lying in front of him on the desk.

"Okay, Mary," the sheriff states, "give me a little bit of time to work on this, and I will be back in touch, and oh, by the way, has anybody else tried to contact you?"

"About Eric, no," Mary comments. "Only my mother called from that police station in Durango. She was using the station's phone. Darren, our neighbor, is now missing. Supposedly, his tires were shot, and it flipped the car that he was driving; his body was not found. Some real funny things are happening, Sheriff. It is crazier than a monkey flying to the moon!"

"Thanks for letting me know the information. I'll check into things. I'm sure the police personnel down there are on top of it," Sheriff Redlock assures her. "I'm sorry, Mary. If anybody else tries to contact you, please let us know right away."

"Will do, thanks, Sheriff, for all your help."

The sheriff escorts Mary out of the building and returns to his office. Sitting down, he glances down at his notepad where his notes about Mary's story are written, tapping the blue pen that he is holding in his right hand repeatedly on it while thinking about Eric's unexpected contact. He abruptly snatches the notepad from the desk and swings his chair in a half circle, standing up, and briskly walking out the office. At a quick pace down the hallway, he turns through an open door into the investigation room. There are four investigators at separate desks. Two are on the phone talking while the other two are staring at their computer screens typing. Their desks are filled with various papers and different colored stickies with handwritten scribblings.

"Jimmy," the sheriff says, getting the attention of one of the investigators, who is at his computer typing. Placing the yellow notepad on Jimmy's desk, the sheriff orders, "We need to find out where this number is right away"—pointing to the number that Mary gave to him—"and I want all the files pulled on a kid named Eric Token!"

"Gotcha," Jimmy says. He writes on a sticky the number and states, "Give me a little bit."

"Let me know when you have it." Sheriff Redlock states and picks up his notepad from the messy desk. He turns and starts walking out, saying to the investigators, "And clean this pigpen up!"

"Will do, sir!" Jimmy responds in a respectful manner.

Sheriff Redlock goes back to his office. At his desk, he begins to thumb through his notepad, searching for more clues. He makes a few phone calls, and a half an hour of time passes. Jimmy appears at the sheriff's door, saying, "Sir, we got it."

"Good," the sheriff says.

"It is a motel room number in Phoenix," Jimmy declares.

"What is the number to that motel?"

Jimmy walks into the office and places on the sheriff's desk a green folder tagged "Eric Token" with a sticky note placed on top with the name and number of the motel. He glances down at the sticky; it reads, "Heaven's Place and More."

Larry quickly glances up at Jimmy and says, "Are you pulling my leg with a stunt like this?"

"Hilarious, isn't it?" Jimmy remarks.

"Different, man!"

"Different is good, right?" Jimmy says and then clearly states, "Sir, everything is in the folder."

The sheriff nods, and Jimmy turns around, leaving the room. Larry reaches for the phone, dialing the motel's phone number.

"Hello and good afternoon. Heaven's Place and More Motel, this is Raul. How can I help you?"

"Raul, this is Sheriff Larry Redlock outside of Denver, Colorado. I am on a case of possibly two missing persons, a couple, and we think they might have stayed at your place last night. It was a young man of thirty-four years old and a woman in her early thirties. He is six foot and two inches with brown hair, brown eyes, and big through the shoulders; she is five foot and six inches with red hair and blue eyes." He pauses to give Raul time to process the information and then continues, "Does this ring a bell at all, or do you remember a couple staying with you around this description?"

Raul thinks and looks over at his booking records to refresh his memory. He says, "Sheriff, yeah, a couple stayed here that were probably around that age and possible description if I remember correctly—they paid cash and said their names were Mr. and Mrs. Dubois."

"Did they check out this morning?"

"Yeah, however, they did not officially check out, but left this morning."

"Okay, thanks," says the sheriff, gratefully. "Do you remember anything else about them?"

Raul thinks, and as he is about to say no, a thought comes to his mind, quickly commenting, "Actually, I remember that the guy came in early this morning and paid for some time to use the telephone—he paid cash, I think."

"Okay, anything else? Maybe something after cleaning their room—did they leave anything behind?"

"No, I don't think so. I think that was it, pretty uneventful, seemed like nice folks."

"Well, Raul," Larry sincerely says, "I really appreciate your time, and I might be getting in touch with you again if I have more questions."

"No problem, here to help!" Raul cheerfully states.

"Thanks again," Sheriff Redlock says with appreciation.

As Raul is about to say goodbye, he remembers that they found a note behind the front cover of the Bible in the nightstand. "Oh, Sheriff, wait," Raul hurriedly says.

"Yes," Sheriff Redlock states.

"I just remembered that my wife, who was cleaning the room, found a handwritten note in the Bible that we leave for guests to read in the rooms. Wait a second, my wife kept it and placed it somewhere around here because it was quite strange."

"Different?" Sheriff Redlock asks.

"Different, for sure."

"Go figure," Larry remarks in a sly tone.

Raul leaves the phone and returns, stating, "Got it."

"Good."

"Okay," Raul says, "it reads: 'Need to find the ones we love, so we can love the ones we find. The key is in the hole, but the key has not turned.'" Raul pauses and then says, "Then it reads as initials or something: 'P. B.'"

Larry pauses, thinking what the note might mean and then asks, "Anything else on that note, Raul?"

"No, that is it."

"Raul, okay. Please place that note in a safe spot and we will probably be reaching out later. Thanks for the help. If anything else comes up, please let us know."

"We are here to help, sir!" Raul says with generous hospitality.

"Have a good day, Raul."

"You, too."

Larry hangs up the phone and makes a few more phone calls. He then grabs the yellow notepad and green folder from off the desk and stands up, leaving the office. Blazing through the hallway and while passing an office to his left, he shouts, "Sergeant Jones, we are on the move!"

Sergeant Jones, a stocky woman with short, curly blonde hair and dark, green eyes, comes zooming out of the office with a duffle bag in hand. She catches up to Sheriff Redlock, and, walking side by side, they jolt out of the building and into the sheriff's vehicle, racing out of the parking lot.

STANDING in front of Tracy's big white house and alongside of him is Burt and a nurse with a stretcher next to her. Stan and the boys pull up to the house with Darren lying unconscious in the back seat with an IV in his arm. Tracy opens the vehicle's back door, and Stan states, "He's in a coma." Cautiously, they remove Darren from the vehicle and place him on the stretcher, taking him inside. Wheeling Darren next to the living room and into the lounge, they lift him off the stretcher and onto a movable bed. The nurse checks his vitals and places a new IV into his arm. She states with assurance, "He'll be okay."

Tracy orders Burt, "Go get Syrup." Burt leaves the room. Tracy then says to the nurse, "Can you please give me a minute?" She obeys his wish and walks out of the room. He steps towards the bedside, watching Darren breathe slowly in and out. His eyes notice Darren's fist clinched tightly below. Wondering what is inside, he reaches down and starts gently prying Darren's fingers open. As they reluctantly move backwards and with the unpeeling of the last finger, the medallion is unwrapped. Tracy stands with astonishment glaring down at it, thinking, After all these years it is right in front of me—forty years searching. Reverently, he picks up the medallion from Darren's imprinted hand and places it in his right front pant pocket. As he closes Darren's fingers shut, both Burt and Syrup enter the room. Standing at the bedside, looking down at Darren's limp body, Syrup notices his closed fist and the reddening through the fingers, glancing up at Tracy. Tracy stands, staring down at Darren, in awe of what is in his own pant pocket. Syrup then asks, "Do you mind stepping back a bit?" Tracy looks down at Syrup, for he is almost a foot taller than him, and then takes a few steps back. Moving in front of Darren's fist and opening it, Syrup sees a round red indentation mark in his hand, as if something circular had been held very tightly. He looks up at Tracy, and Tracy is now looking down at him nodding his head slightly up and down, gesturing, that yes, indeed, he has the medallion. Without anything said, Tracy turns and walks out of the room with Syrup and Burt following him.

They all walk down a hallway and into a locked study. The room is walled with dark cherrywood bookshelves filled with ancient scrolls and antique books; an African ebonywood desk sits in the middle with a small black table lamp on the corner; there are three large, puffy, black chairs, one behind and two in front of the desk; hanging on the back wall is an enormous map of the world. Tracy walks and stands behind the desk next to the chair. Syrup and Burt both sit on the edge of the two chairs in front of the desk. Tracy reaches into his right pocket and gradually pulls out the medallion. He sits down in the chair and places his closed hand, with his fingers facing upward, on top of the desk. He slowly opens his hand, revealing the medallion's silver, aged appearance. Syrup and Burt lean over on the edge of the chairs as all three stare down at it, marveling at its perfectly crafted handwork. They remain in silence as Tracy lays it on the desk for further examination. He reaches down inside a desk drawer and pulls out a magnifying glass, placing it next to the medallion. Syrup automatically stands up and takes a step forward, leaning on the edge of the desk to look directly down over it. He grabs the magnifying glass and places it four inches from the medallion, investigating its markings. He reaches down and turns the medallion over, studying the back. After thorough review, Syrup places the medallion and magnifying glass back onto the desk. He stands straight up and nods up and down to Tracy, signifying its authenticity.

W EARING hats and sunglasses in order to be masked, Eric and Cassie sit silently in a rental car down the street and around the corner from where they followed Sam, Tip, Jay, and the others before watching them go up the hillside. The couple knows that if they continue waiting much longer, they will eventually be spotted and become hunted like sitting ducks in a pond. However, due to the heat and unpreparedness of the situation, the next best logical proposition is to hike up the hillside, which seems extremely risky and acutely dangerous. Eric, not wanting to sit in the car anymore, comments, "Alright, we should probably get going."

With her eyes explicitly shouting "No way," Cassie understands that they should get moving, and so she agreeably responds, "I know."

They step out of the car with their water bottles in hand and walk to the bottom of the hill. Eric reaches down and takes Cassie's hand as they start the ascent. After winding back and forth through the low, dense pinon trees for thirty minutes, interspersed with water breaks, they see a big black metal gate up ahead spanning in both directions, protecting someone's private property.

Eric moves his head slightly upward, as if stretching to hear something from the distance. Coming towards them is a faint sound of tires rustling on a dirt road and a diesel motor purring. "A truck is coming," Eric quietly mentions. They both hide behind a tree, hearing the truck pass by them as it travels down the hillside. Silence again ensues, and Eric states, "Let's keep moving."

Cautiously walking upwards, they become more careful with their movements. When they reach a stone's throw from the gate, they stop and see the dirt road beyond it where the truck was traveling, followed by some rough brush further in. They decide to follow the gate further up the hill. Hiking another half mile, Eric quickly comes to a halt with Cassie stopping beside him. He points up past the gate to a green, manicured lawn and the back of Tracy's mansion and cautions her, "Shhhh, look up there." Cassie looks and whispers, "Wow, unbelievable." They quickly hide behind another tree and listen for anything peculiar. Eric scans the area for cameras, noticing nothing. He then bends down and picks up a tiny rock and throws it at the fence, checking for electricity or an alarm. The rock bounces off the fence with no sound or alarm blaring. He thinks, Thank goodness. "Wait here," he says to Cassie and intuitively maneuvers closer to the fence. Stopping with his back against a tree's trunk which lies between him and the fence, he slowly pokes his head around to take a closer look at the premises. One hundred feet before Tracy's white house lies an outbuilding. Eric hides back behind the tree and motions to Cassie to move towards him.

Cassie carefully walks up to him and presses her body against his chest. He embraces her and whispers into her ear, "Things look clear." He pauses and continues, "There is a building before the house. We will go for that." Then he points to a nearby stump lying on the ground and says, "Let's roll that up to the fence and use it to jump over—you first and then I'll follow."

Cassie, feeling proud of her heroic husband, grins because he never seems afraid of anything—containing a relentless grit and stubbornness, for good and bad.

Eric moves to the stump, and, squatting down, he rolls it over to the fence. Eric instructs, "Here, you get on first, jump, and grab the top. I'll push you up and over." Cassie follows his directions, crawling over the fence and falling to the ground unharmed. Then, Eric takes a deep, long breath, stepping onto the stump. He jumps and grabs the top of the fence with both hands, and with great effort, he lifts himself up and over, rolling as he lands. Cassie rushes over to him and reaches down, asking, "Are you okay?" Eric expresses joyfully with a huge smile, "Couldn't feel any better."

Eric stands up, and together they both run, ducked and bent over, toward the back of the outbuilding. When they reach the back corner of it, they hear voices from inside. Eric decides to crawl to one of the small back windows in the middle of the building, wanting to hear better what is being said:

"I don't know where they are," a familiar man's voice remarks.

"Yes, you do, and you better start talking!" another man's deep voice commands.

"I don't, and even if I did, I wouldn't be telling you guys anyways."

Eric moves back to the corner where Cassie is waiting. He whispers, "I think we found him."

Her face winces with question to his vague declaration of "him."

"I think he is in this building."

Her face again stares at him with wonder, not knowing who he is referring to.

"My father," Eric announces indefinitely, "we found him."

Cassie's eyes pop wide open with surprise, but then says, "If we don't quickly get out of here, we aren't finding anyone."

"You're right again, Sherlock," Eric states. "We better get out of here."

Kneeling down, holding each other's hands, they both glance around, hoping to find a more secure place to hide. Seeing a small tool shed twenty-five feet away, they both look at each other, knowing that this is where they should go. In hand, they stand and turn the corner, bolting for the shed. Arriving at the door, Eric hurriedly opens it, and they slide in, unnoticed.

"WHERE are we going?" Sergeant Gentry Jones asks Sheriff Larry Redlock as they drive down the freeway.

"Heading to Phoenix," Larry replies.

"Phoenix, Arizona?" Sergeant Jones asks in confusion.

"Yes," Sheriff states, "Arizona." He glances over to witness Gentry's facial expression of total unbelief, and then says, "We got to go see someone."

"Who is in Arizona?" she asks.

"Someone that might know a little bit about what we are looking for."

"And what are we looking for?"

"So," Sheriff Redlock says, "A long time ago there was a boy that was missing, and this boy's name was Eric."

Gentry notices the sheriff's facial genuineness, knowing that what he is saying must mean a great deal to him. Otherwise, why go to Arizona? She asks, "Okay, what is the importance of this boy?"

The sheriff begins, saying, "I had a boy his age when he went missing. My boy's name was Edward. He was seventeen years old at the time and, well, ya know, sometimes things don't always go as planned." He pauses and continues, "Edward died in a car accident three weeks later with some friends."

Gentry gasps, "I'm so sorry. I never knew this about you."

"Yeah, not many people do."

"How?"

Before responding, the sheriff thinks about his son's death, remembering his beauty and the wonderful love that he felt for him, and still does. Without responding directly to the question, he then says, "Sometimes it is too hard."

"I can only imagine," Gentry expresses, sympathetically.

"Yeah, I never really talk about it much," Larry states. "Edward was a good boy, a little emotional and crazy at times, but what teenager isn't?"

"You got that right."

"It was too painful for me to talk much about."

"I bet."

"It eventually broke the spirit of my wife," Larry mentions. "She couldn't take it that our only son died, and I lost her, emotionally and mentally, for many years—I, too, was lost in my own way for many years as well." He then abruptly asks Gentry, "You know what?"

"What?"

"I don't know if you ever really come around from losing a child prematurely; however, something happened to my wife and me some years ago that miraculously helped."

"What happened?" Gentry asks with curiosity.

"What I'm about to tell you stays in this vehicle, okay? I don't want any rumors that I'm a softy, got it?"

"You bet, boss."

"I heard a voice some time ago—a still small voice. It called me "son," grabbing my attention, and then it peacefully asked, 'Where is your heart?'"

Sheriff Redlock's voice lumps in his throat, holding back the fresh, surfacing emotions that this memory stirs in him every time he shares it. Gentry waits patiently for the sheriff to regain his composure. Larry takes a big inhale and exhale and then, wiping his eyes clear, he continues, "That voice then said: 'Your son is okay. He is with me.'"

Allowing the importance of this moment to settle in, Larry pauses, glancing over to Gentry. Then, he says, "At that moment, I knew that my heart was carrying anger and bitterness. My boy was just too young, full of life, and I knew at that moment that I had not let him go yet—you never let them go in some ways, but I had to let him go. At this moment I said okay and accepted what the voice told me; instantaneously, I felt a weight lift off from within my soul and shoulders. It was an incredible sensation."

Gentry's eyes remain glued on him in inspiration, thinking, Wow, what a remarkable experience. Larry then quickly states, "We need to find this kid. We will. Lucy must be reunited with her boy."

"Okay," Gentry replies, still digesting what she has recently heard and trying to understand the true connection that Larry has with Eric and his family and what mission they are actually embarking upon.

"I have," Larry states, "let the others know that we will be away for a while. We will call the jurisdiction down there in Arizona and be on our way personally to see that this situation gets handled correctly. Do you understand, Gentry?"

"Not really," she states honestly, "But my job is to support my boss, and that I can do."

"Lucy is not going to lose her son, okay?"

"Okay," Sergeant Jones affirms. Her phone begins to ring, and she answers, "Hello."

"Gentry, this is Jimmy. Are you with Sheriff?"

"Yes."

"Please tell him that they can't find Eric anywhere. I have reached out to the officers down there and they have been looking for him and no word. Please let him know."

With the phone pressed to her ear, she comments to Larry, "This is Jimmy, and no word on the boy and his wife."

"Okay," Larry says gratefully, "Please ask him if he told them that we are on our way, and does he have the sheriff's contact number down there?"

Gentry follows Larry's orders and asks Jimmy.

"Yes, they know," Jimmy replies. "And the sheriff there is Sheriff York, and this is his phone number." Jimmy relays the contact information to her.

"Great," she says, "Is there anything else?"

"No."

"Okay then, keep us posted if you hear anything else."

"Okay," Jimmy replies and hangs up.

Gentry asks Larry, "Do you want me to contact the sheriff down there to let him know that we are on our way?"

"Yes, please."

Gentry dials the number and begins to speak with Sheriff York. Gentry hands the phone to Larry and says, "He wants to speak with you."

"Hello, Sheriff York?," asks Larry.

"Yes, Sheriff Redlock, what is going on?"

Larry explains to Sheriff York why he and Sergeant Jones are on their way. Larry shortly ends the conversation, saying, "Great. Thanks for understanding, Sheriff, this is our number, and please keep us posted if you find this kid and his wife. We should see you guys soon. Thank you."

THE night begins to fall while Cassie and Eric are cuddled up together sitting on the cement floor in the corner of the tool shed. Eric gently taps her on the shoulder, and as she glances up at him, he signals with his eyes toward the door, gesturing, that it is time to get up and see if it is clear outside to go. Both rise to their feet and tiptoe to the door. Eric slides the door a quarter of the way open and glances out. He then slowly closes the door and gives Cassie, who is standing right behind him, a gentle and smooth kiss. He then hugs her, whispering, "Sweetheart, whatever happens this night, know that my love for you will be forever." Releasing his arms from around her, he lovingly holds her hand and turns around, facing the door, opening it. They rush out to the side of the outbuilding to confirm if indeed it is his father inside.

Reaching the side of the building, they stop and kneel down to the ground listening for any more voices coming from the inside—they hear nothing; however, off to the distance they unexpectedly hear *bark, bark, bark.*

"Oh no, guard dogs," Cassie whispers.

They rapidly move to the front door, which is unlocked, and quietly enter. Inside is a small living room to the right that has tan carpet, two red couches, and a television stand. Behind the living room is a small kitchen with a hallway leading to three smaller bedrooms and a single bathroom. They hear a faint rumble come from one of the bedrooms.

Cautiously, they walk forward to the hallway and turn down it. A mumble sound comes from the last the door on the left. As they reach the door and carefully turn the handle, opening the door, inside is a man lying on the ground face down with a rag gagged in his mouth and hands tied behind his back. Eric and Cassie enter the room and close the door.

Eric walks to the man and rolls him over. When Eric sees the man's face, he says with joy, but quietly, so not to be heard, "Father." Eric hurriedly frees Daryl, and they embrace as father and son.

"My son," Daryl says, panting for air.

"Dad," Eric says, "I'm so glad to see you."

"Me, too," Daryl expresses with happiness.

Cassie moves over to them, and Daryl glances up at her with question.

"Dad," Eric says, "This is my wife, Cassie."

Daryl, feeling exhausted, slowly reaches out his hand, asking Cassie to bend down and join the embracing. She kneels down and they all three hug each other.

"It is so wonderful to meet you," Daryl whispers in her ear. "You, too," Cassie gracefully says with delight, as she embraces her new father-in-law and now, instantly, has more family.

Eric swiftly says, "Dad, I have so much to tell you after so much time, but I don't think we should stay here too much longer."

"Good idea," Daryl says, agreeable.

"Can you stand up?" Eric asks his weak father.

"I think so."

Eric reaches down and with both arms helps his father to his feet. Daryl stands up with extreme dehydration and fatigue, resting his arm over Eric's shoulder for stability. Daryl says with tiredness, "There are three of them. They come in every so often, and then I think they leave because I don't hear anything for a while."

"Are you sure you are okay to get out of here, Dad?" Eric asks.

"Just needed a good shoulder to rest on."

Eric smiles, saying, "You will always have one."

"Thank you, son," Daryl states.

Eric then says, "There is a fence outside that we will have to jump over to clear the premises."

Daryl quickly interrupts, "We can't leave yet. They have Darren in the main house."

"Who is Darren?" asks Eric, never hearing the name before.

"A dear friend and neighbor. The men have mentioned his name, and it appears that he is in another house close by."

"Yes, there is a big house, mansion-like, outside," Eric states. "But Dad, if we go in there, there may be no way out."

"Son," Daryl says, gasping and with conviction, "we aren't leaving without Darren."

"Alright, Dad, wherever we go from here, we go together."

The three of them walk out of the room and down the hallway to the front door. Before leaving, they wait for a moment to hear any voices or guard dogs barking close by. Hearing nothing, Cassie warily opens the door and glances outside, saying, "It's clear." They leave the outbuilding, moving toward the main house. The guard dogs begin to bark behind them from a distance. "Hurry," Eric says while they rush to a back door and enter the house.

Standing in a white hallway with dark blue trim are various Vincent van Gogh paintings hanging on the wall. With Daryl still draped over Eric's shoulder for support and Cassie in front of them, they begin to walk down the hallway. At the end of it, it opens to a living room. There sit Tracy, Burt, Syrup, Packet, Jay, Sam, Tip, Charlie, Stan, and their crews.

"We've been watching you," Tracy frankly says. "Please come in and take a seat. You have come at the perfect time."

The three watchfully enter the room and sit down on an open couch that is parallel to Tracy. Burt and Syrup are sitting on the other couch, while the others are sitting on wooden chairs spaced around the room.

Tracy asks, "Eric, this is your name, right?"

"Yes," he replies.

"We've had a hard time catching you," Tracy mentions as he glances at Cassie.

"Daryl," Tracy then says, "it is good of you to join us, too."

Tracy then states to Eric, "We need something that we believe you either have or know where it is." He pauses, waiting for him to respond. Eric stoically stares at Tracy, suggesting that he will not offer any information. Tracy waits for a few more seconds, then reaches down to an ash tray sitting next to him and picks up his cigar—taking a few big inhales, then puffing out the smoke right in front of them. With his legs crossed like a business executive, he then places the cigar back into the tray and leans back into the couch, appearing relaxed. His eyes move over to Burt, Jay, Packet, and the others, and with a hint of a grin he directly says to Eric, "Let me put it as straight as I can with you: we know you know where it is. We ask you first, politely, to please offer it up."

Eric does not respond.

"Eric," Tracy states with emphasis, "Are you sure you want to go down this road?"

Eric thinks of Cassie and Daryl. He knows that if he does not say or do something, they are most likely going to be in peril. He then remarks, "On one condition."

Suddenly, in the next room over, the lounge, Darren's eyes gradually open as he gains consciousness—blur turns to color, color turns to form, and form turns to reality. He asks himself, Where am I and how did I get here? Feeling fatigued, yet exerting all his effort, he raises his head, then next his shoulders, which raises his torso to a sitting position, slouching over as he droops with weakness. Glancing down at his left hand, he sees a circular red imprint in his palm and a picture bursts into his mind: a small boy with stark, brown eyes and straight, black hair sits on a blanket. The boy is playing with a medallion in his hand. There is a light that is shining from the bottom of the blanket; its rays ascend upward around the boy. The boy looks over to him with angry eyes. The picture then vanishes from his mind.

Darren thinks, Oh, a medallion, yes, that medallion, the one the boy was playing with—I had it. However, something doesn't seem right with the boy's eyes. Why was he angry in such an illuminous moment? What is that boy telling me? I must get up. Do I have the strength? Darren hears dim voices in the other room. I need to get out of here, he thinks. Okay, legs, let's get moving, get me out of here. He begins to shuffle his legs, moving them inch by inch until both legs are thrown off the bed's edge, dangling in the air, swinging back and forth like pendulums in a grandfather clock. With his head hanging down over his chest, he remains hunched over like an unused accordion as his arms brace his body's weight from tumbling forward to the floor; he breathes heavily. Resting for a moment, he starts to slightly lift his head, glancing around the room for a phone, someone to call for help, because he awkwardly senses that he is not in a safe place. He begins to feel light-headed. Like an avalanche crashing down from a steep mountain's face, Darren passes out and his body free-falls to the tiled floor below—*thump*, his head smacks the ground.

The others in the living room hear the loud sound, and Tracy shouts, "Oh, my gosh! Syrup, hurry! Burt, call Maria right away!"

Tracy and Syrup run into the lounge. Burt runs toward the kitchen, yelling, "Maria, Maria, help!" Jay stands up and points a gun at Eric, Cassie, and Daryl. The other men stand up, sticking their chests out in a puff, like military infantry ready to enter the roaring battle at the commander's signal.

Inside the lounge, Darren's body lies twisted on the floor with his limbs in all directions as dark, red blood is pooling all over the tile from a cracked skull. Maria, the nurse, scurries into the room. "Hurry! Hurry!" Tracy exclaims. Seeing the emergency, Maria goes right to work, grabbing a towel from the closet and applying pressure to the wound. Researching the cut with her fingers, she says to Tracy, "Sir, it's not as bad as it looks."

In the other room a gun is fired—*bang, bang*. Tracy turns and runs into the living room. Eric lies motionless on the floor, bleeding from two gunshot wounds to the side. Cassie is draped over him, crying, "Oh, no, no! Eric! No!" Jay is holding a smoking gun. Tracy shouts in anger, "What have you done? We need him!" He yells for the nurse, "Maria, in here now, hurry!"

Maria wraps Darren's head with the towel and lays it onto the ground, running into the living room. She bends down next to Eric and checks the gun wound. Concerned, she says, "It looks bad. I don't know if I can handle this on my own. It would be best to get him to a hospital."

Tracy screams to the men, "Get him wrapped up and to the nearest hospital—make sure he lives!"

Charlie and his crew peel Cassie off Eric's limp body as she screams, "Let me go! Get your dirty hands off me! Let me be with my husband!"

Daryl fiercely glares at Jay as if he is about to charge him, saying with rage, "You no-good scoundrel!"

Burt points a gun at Daryl and says, "Don't try it. Stay put."

The men take Cassie and Daryl down the hall and lock them into a room. Cassie bangs and bangs on the door, yelling, "Let me out of here! You cowards!"

Tracy orders Jay, Tip, and Sam, "Fast, get him to the hospital!"

They pick up Eric and carry him to the SUV that is parked in front. They place Eric in the back seat, and with towels Jay tries to stop as much bleeding as he can. They speed off.

Back inside the house, Tracy asks Burt, "What happened?"

"Eric stood up," Burt responds, "and was acting like he was about to run, and so Jay popped him twice."

"So what? Why shoot him?" Tracy asks angrily. "Don't we have men to catch him?"

"Yeah," Burt replies, "Not sure why he did what he did."

"We better hope that he lives so we can get what we need."

SAM screeches to a halt at the Phoenix Hospital emergency room. Two doctors wearing dark blue scrubs and pushing a stretcher come dashing through the sliding glass door entrance. Tip steps out of the passenger side of the vehicle and opens the back door. Covered in blood, Jay is pressing a towel to Eric's side.

As the doctors reach the car, one doctor asks, "He's been shot in the side, right?"

"Yes, please help my friend," Jay responds, trying to be as sincere as possible.

"We'll do our best," the other doctor says as they place Eric on the stretcher and wheel him inside to a prepared surgical room. Jay follows them in and stops at the front desk, watching the doors close. A female nurse walks up to Jay and politely asks, "Sir, was that your friend?"

"Yes."

"So sorry," she states.

"That's okay."

"Sir," she says, "We will need some information on your friend. Will this be okay?"

"Sure thing."

The nurse walks behind the front desk, and while sitting behind a computer, she asks Jay, "What is your friend's name?"

"Eric."

"His last name?"

"Tolbert," Jay says, knowing that he is lying.

"How old is Eric and what happened to him?"

"He is thirty-four years old, and he got shot in the side."

"What happened?"

"He and another one of our friends were playing around with a gun and it accidently shot him."

"You are the contact person for Eric?"

"Yes, ma'am, I am."

"What is your name, sir?"

"Carl Johnson."

"And your contact information, Carl?"

Jay gives the nurse his phone number, but a fake address.

"Okay, thanks, Carl," the nurse says. "Are you going to be waiting here?"

"Yes."

"Okay, we will come for you once we know Eric's situation. In the meantime, there are some clean clothes you can change into," she says while pointing to a rack full of shirts and pants. "You can clean up in the bathroom, and inside there is a plastic bag to put your dirty clothes into."

"Thanks, ma'am," Jay says and leaves the desk, going to the bathroom. He washes up and puts on new clothes. He leaves the emergency room and enters the waiting area, picking up his phone and calling Tip.

"Hey, where are you guys?" he asks.

"Hey mate-o," Tip answers, "We are waiting outside in the car."

"I will be in here for a little bit," Jay expresses and abruptly hangs up, not wanting to talk. He finds an empty seat, and while sitting down Burt calls him, asking, "Jay, what's the status?"

"They are operating on him right now."

"Okay, keep us posted."

"Gotcha."

Ending the call, Jay places his phone onto his lap while being on the alert, having a strange feeling that someone is watching him. However, as he glances around, he only notices people appearing exhausted and worried as they wait, hopefully, for some good news. Agitated nonetheless, he swiftly stands up from the chair and goes to the front of the hospital, watching closely his surroundings. Reaching the entrance, the automatic doors open and he steps out, peering to his right and left, noticing nothing alarming. Turning to walk back inside, a small man with a round face, dark brown skin, and bluish-green eyes stands in front of him. Jay pauses and looks down at the man. The man says, "Excuse me, sir, I noticed that you suddenly stood up and walked out of the waiting area. Are you okay?"

"Who are you?" Jay inquires with heavy speculation.

"I hope you are okay, sir," the man responds without clearly answering the question. "I have a daughter in the emergency room, and she is fighting for her life. She is ten years old and has cancer."

"I'm sorry about that," Jay kindly offers his condolences.

"Thank you," the man says. "She is tough. This morning she woke up in bed and was having a hard time breathing, and it got worse and worse, so we rushed her to the hospital. We have been here the whole morning and afternoon. I was just sitting in the waiting area catching a little breather, needing some time to ponder and think on my own life. My wife is in the room with our baby girl."

"Is she going to be okay?" Jay asks, not wanting to be rude.

"I think so," the man positively states.

"I sure hope so."

"Why are you here?" the man inquires.

"Someone that I know was shot."

"Oh no, is he going to be alright?"

"Well, not sure, but we are hoping for the best."

"God willing," the man says kindly. "Let's hope that both your friend and my daughter are healed."

"Yeah, let's hope," Jay says, not believing in any diety.

"Good to meet you," the man states in a friendly tone.

Jay responds, "You, too."

The man turns and walks away through the doors. Jay doubts the man's sincerity and takes a few cautious steps forward. With his foot in motion, he hears a voice in his mind: "Your life will change very soon." He thinks, What the devil does this mean? Stepping forward, a picture of his only daughter shoots into his mind like lightning spontaneously striking an electric pole, splitting it in two. It has been thirty years since he last saw her. Uncontrollably, his emotions are flooded with feelings of longing to see her tender face, glowing blue skylight eyes, and the random freckles that paint her face with creative uniqueness. In a daydreaming daze, he walks back to the emergency room.

Passing through the waiting room doors, he heads to the front desk to check on Eric's status as another thought enters his mind: "It is time to find the ones you love." The longing feeling to see his daughter now ruptures in his soul like a volcano finally exploding with unbearable heat, sensing a sudden urge to get out of there. In perplexed emotions, Jay asks the nurse at the desk with tremendous impatience, "How is Eric doing?"

The nurse glances up from the desk and says, "Sir, we just spoke a few minutes ago. Please give it some time. I know it is difficult to wait, but please be patient outside, and we will come find you once we know his status, okay?"

Jay's phone rings, and it is Burt.

"Hey, we are on our way," Burt says in a hurried tone. "Darren took a turn for the worse, and so we need more help. Stay put and we will see you guys in a while."

"Gotcha."

Jay hangs up and asks the nurse almost in a panic, "Any news on him?"

"Sir," the nurse states, "they are still working on him."

"What does this mean?"

"It has been difficult," the nurse says. "The wounds were severe, and he lost a lot of blood. This is all I can tell you right now. They are working hard to stabilize him. Now, sir, please wait in the waiting area."

Not able to stand still, Jay leaves to go outside to get some fresh air, hoping to clear his mind. He pulls out a cigar from his front pant pocket and starts smoking, wondering where his daughter could possibly be.

Jay begins to pace back in forth with an idea coming to his mind—Call Reggie, his old business associate. Knowing he has not spoken to Reggie in years and not sure if he has him in his phone contacts anymore, he scrolls through the names—it is still there. He dials the number.

"Hello," a man's voice says.

"Reggie Bateman?" Jay inquires.

"Who's calling?" the man asks.

"It's Jay." There is a long pause at the end of the line.

"Red, Jay Murphy?"

"Yup."

"No way."

"Is this Reggie?" Jay asks.

"You bet, you old duffer." Reggie shouts.

"It has been a while."

"You bet, what's up?"

"I know it has been some time," Jay says, "but I might need your help with something."

"Red, you good ol' boy, you can count on me."

"Reggie, my daughter, you knew her, right?" Jays asks.

"Red, that was some time ago," Reggie states. "Gosh, she must have been a little pup, maybe four or five years old."

"Yeah," Jay confirms, "and I've not seen her for a while. I need to find her. You knew her aunt, Linda, right?"

"Yeah, your sister-in-law."

"Yes," Jay mentions. "I haven't spoken to her for years since my brother died, and nobody knows or has heard a thing about her since then."

"That was a tough one, Red."

"Yup." Jay comments, "Linda took care of him for a while, but left after it got so bad."

"Alright," Reggie states, "For you Red, I'll make a few phone calls. It's been some years since I've talked to those folks; let me see what I can find out. I'll call you back."

Jay says gratefully, "Okay, thanks, Reg."

"Red, are you doing okay, man?" Reggie asks with his curiosity spiked.

"Doing okay, thanks, Reg."

Not pushing for more information, Reggie comments, "Okay, Red, let's see if we can find that sweet daughter of yours."

"Thanks, talk to you soon," Jay says and hangs up the phone, watching a black SUV pull up into the hospital and head toward the emergency room sliding door entrance—it is Burt with Darren.

S HERIFF Redlock and Sergeant Jones are an hour away from the Phoenix hospital, and Sheriff Tim York calls.

Larry answers the phone, "Hello, Sheriff York, is this you?"

"Yes," Sheriff York says, "Wanted to let you know that we are taking a look into a lead."

"Great."

"We posted Eric and his wife's picture on our missing persons profile link and the hospital in downtown Phoenix gave us a call. They think a patient resembles the picture of Eric, and some are actually saying that he was in there the other morning with his wife after a freak accident."

"Not a good couple days for him," Sherrif Redlock mentions.

"Yeah, I'm not sure what that is all about," Tim says, "but we also received a call from an international number, registered to a local coffee shop in Uruguay, saying that there might be another missing person in the hospital named Darren Brown. Do you know a man named Darren Brown that is missing also?"

Sherrif Redlock answers enthusiastically, "Yes, he is missing along with Eric. It is quite a long story."

"Alright," Tim says, "We are on our way right now."

"Sounds great," Larry states. "We will head to the hospital. Let us know if things shift."

"Okay," comments Tim, "We will let you know how these things go."

"Okay, thank you," Larry graciously says.

Tim ends the call, and with two other officers they shortly arrive at the Phoenix hospital. After some dialogue with hospital security and other staff, Sheriff York and the other officers are escorted to the post-surgery unit. Standing at the door, they get buzzed in. A nurse welcomes them: "Hello, he is over here—Eric Tolbert."

Entering into the hospital room where Eric lies, they stop at the end of the bed. Tim then walks around the bed, moving closer in an effort to get a better view of Eric's face through the tube that is stuck down his throat and the oxygen mask that is over his mouth and nose.

The nurse then says, "It might help if you could see his face, huh?" Sheriff York nods yes, and she pulls the mask up into the air. Tim squints his eyes, focusing more intently on the pale facial features. He pulls out of his pocket a colored picture of Eric, lifting it up to compare. Glancing back and forth from the picture to Eric, he finally deems with confidence, "Yup, it is him."

The nurse softly lays the mask back on Eric's face and respectfully waits for him to give her any more direction. Tim graciously says, "Ma'am, thanks, that's all we need right now." The nurse leaves the room, and Sheriff York says to Officer Wright, a stout man in his middle forties, "Call it in."

They walk outside the hospital room and Sheriff York demands to hospital security, "We need to get the hospital locked down right away."

One of the security guards responds with urgency, grabbing the radio from his belt and yelling into it, "Code red! Code red! Code red!"

In short order, all hospital personnel respond rapidly moving through the hallways, closing doors, checking windows, searching closets, and sweeping through the various floors with practiced efficiency to shut everything down like a tight water drum with stringent security measurements in place—every eye closely watching for suspicious activity.

Returning to the hospital from a nearby convenience store picking up sodas and smokes, Jay cautions to the others in the SUV, "We better not go back there."

"Why not?" Burt, riding in the front passenger seat, questions.

"If we go back, we risk getting caught."

Sam, who is driving, nods his head in agreement. Tip is sitting next to Jay and says sarcastically, "Well, bud-o, you might already be in trouble."

"How?" Jay asks, innocently.

"You a redcoat, mate-o?" Tip accuses.

"What do you mean?"

"Burt-o, want to tell him?"

Burt stares ahead and states, "Jay, we might have a slight problem on our hands." He pauses and continues, "Jay, do you know somebody in Uruguay?"

"No," Jay answers with conviction.

"Well," Burt states, "As we were waiting in the gas station, Tracy called and said that we should come back to the place because he got tipped that the hospital was being locked down because someone had called from Uruguay saying that Darren was in the hospital."

"I don't know anyone in Uruguay!" Jay cries.

"Are you sure you haven't talked with anyone?" Burt asks, not trusting him.

"No."

"We'll see," Burt remarks, continuing to look forward as they turn and begin to drive to Tracy's place in silence.

Upon arrival, Burt says to Tip, referring to Jay, "Handcuff him."

"What?" Jay exclaims.

Tip pulls out handcuffs and reaches over to take Jay's arm. He pulls it away and sternly says, "You're out of your goshdarn mind!"

Tip sternly says, "You'll put these on-o, bud-o."

Jay responds, "Over my long and lanky dead body!"

Burt pulls out his gun and points it at Jay.

"Really, Burt? Come on." Jay shouts.

"Put them on." Burt commands.

Jay quickly snatches the handcuffs from Tip's hands and places them on his wrists.

"Good boy-o," Tip says with a smile.

"Now," Burt says, "Slowly and calmly, inside."

They exit the vehicle, and with Jay walking in front, they all enter the house. Going down the hallway to the living room, they sit down on the couches with Burt sitting across from Jay while leaving a couch open for Tracy to enter and sit on. Jay glances down to the white carpet below to see if there are any remains of Eric's blood, and there are no stains, appearing brand new.

Tracy walks in with a cigar in his hand and directly asks, "Burt, what do you know?"

Burt answers, "He says he knows nothing."

"Well, it figures," Tracy says. He sits down and comments to Jay, "How about this?" He pauses and then continues, "I never thought that this would take place."

Jay remains quiet and stares at Burt with consternation.

"So," Tracy says, "What do you know about the phone call from Uruguay?"

Jay continues staring at Burt with anger and replies, heatedly, "Nothing!"

"Jay," Burt says, "You have to know something. Who else would give a tip or know anything from South America?"

It suddenly dawns on Tracy that he hasn't seen Syrup or Packet for a while. Tracy interrupts the line of questioning and shouts to the elderly maid, "Consuela, anyone seen Syrup?"

Consuela enters the room and respectfully replies, "No, sir."

Tracy stands up and nervously peers out the large back windows, wondering if they might be outside. Tracy yells to the maid, "Have everyone look for him now." He pauses and then shouts, "And where is Packet?" The maid shakes her head no and shrugs her shoulders, not knowing where he is either. "Find him, too!" Tracy orders.

He moves toward Sam and Tip and commands, "You guys with me. Burt you stay here with Jay. If there is any funny business with him, take care of it."

Tracy leaves the room with Tip and Sam following him. Burt remarks to Jay, "You better hope that the snitch did not come from you."

Jay is about to say something in return when Tip comes running back into the room, saying to Burt, "Go lock him up with the others. Tracy wants everybody on the search."

S HERIFF Redlock and Sergeant Jones arrive to the Phoenix hospital, parking their vehicle near the front entrance. Walking through the parking lot, Sheriff Redlock thinks about his son, saying to himself, "This is for you, kid." At the entrance there is a police officer standing outside the door. Sheriff Redlock flashes his badge to the officer and says, "I'm Sheriff Larry Redlock, and this is Sergeant Gentry Jones. We are from Colorado, and we've been talking with Sheriff York."

The officer talks into his radio and then states, "Go inside and wait. Sheriff York will be down in a few minutes."

Larry and Gentry walk through the entrance door and wait at the front desk. A few minutes after, Sheriff York comes around the corner, and upon seeing the two of them, he asks, "Sheriff Redlock?"

"Yes," Larry responds and then asks in similar fashion, "Sheriff York?"

"Yes, sir, Tim."

They shake hands and Larry introduces Gentry. Tim then states, "This must be a special case for you to come all the way down here."

"Like I said on the phone," Larry responds, "this one is more personal than anything."

"Come this way," Sheriff York expresses, "I'll take you to them."

They walk to and enter an elevator, reaching the fourth floor. The elevator stops, and they step out, walking to the intensive care unit. After being buzzed in, Sheriff York states, "Darren is recovering quite well." He pauses and then continues somberly, "As for the youngster, it is more touch-and-go. The shot wounds have been complicated."

They reach Eric's room first and enter. Sheriff York steps aside, allowing Larry and Gentry to walk up closer. Eric lies with wires coming from his limp body that are connected to the bedside monitor, an oxygen mask, and an IV bag hanging above. Sheriff Redlock thinks about his son because he looked the same before he passed away from complications. The sheriff's emotions begin to swell within him for justice as he walks closer to Eric. Stopping and standing above him, Larry reaches down and holds Eric's hand, whispering to him, "Eric, boy, we will find who did this to you." He backs away and says to Gentry, "Whoever did this to him will pay."

They leave the room and walk next door to see Darren. He is lying in a coma with a white bandage wrapped around a noticeably large bump on his forehead. Larry and Gentry walk in and stop at the end of the bed, gazing down at him, wondering how the puzzle pieces connect. Larry focuses on Darren's facial features because there is something mesmerizing about them, but he doesn't know what exactly. Larry steps to the side of the bed, standing next to Darren, gently reaching down and pulling back the blanket draped over his unconscious body, revealing bare skin from the upper arm to hand. He touches Darren's still flesh, and it's warm, then places the blanket back down.

Sergeant Jones stands witnessing this peculiar and strange behavior from Larry; typically, he is very professional, proper, and courteous until warranted into quick protective action. She thinks, This whole day the sheriff has not been acting himself. However, she brushes her initial feelings aside, giving him the benefit of the doubt.

There is an unusual feeling about Darren that Sheriff Redlock increasingly senses, thus drawing him awkwardly toward Darren, like a child with a puppy—the intrigue and inquiry must be palpable. Larry leans over towards Darren's face, stopping inches away in a paused, hunched-over position, investigating if his eyes are moving behind the shuttered eyelids. Not able to control himself, Larry raises his hand to touch Darren's face, and when his fingers are centimeters away, they swiftly halt, as if hitting an invincible barrier. He then twitches back upwards and stands straight up, staring down at Darren with a baffled gaze, backing away. Larry glances at Gentry with inquisitive eyes and then back down at Darren. Darren's eyes are open and are staring up at him.

To Be Continued . . .